Lights . . . Ca

"Are you the contest winner?" Rod Webb, the director of *Warp Space*, asked, looking at Chet Morton. "Why aren't you in costume? We've got to get rolling here!"

"My sister, Iola, won the contest," Chet said. "She's in makeup."

"Terrific," said Webb, meaning just the opposite. He glanced around and sniffed the air. "Is one of you smoking? There's no smoking on the set."

"Not us," Joe said. "We're tobacco free. But that stuntman . . ."

"Wait a minute, Joe," Frank said. "I smell it, too, and it's not cigarettes."

From behind the hill beyond camp, black smoke billowed into the morning sky. Then small tongues of orange flame danced atop the nearby ridge.

Chet gasped. "Fire!"

THE HARDY BOYS®

TROUBLE IN WARP SPACE

FRANKLIN W. DIXON

SCHOLASTIC INC.

New York Toronto London Auckland Sydney
Mexico City New Delhi Hong Kong Buenos Aires

Contents

1 Location: Space

"I don't know, guys," Chet Morton said. "This doesn't look much like outer space to me." He pressed his nose close to the car window and peered out into the early-morning dusty parking lot.

"You're not taking into account the magic of special effects," Frank Hardy replied with a smile. He pulled the van into a gravel-covered parking space and turned off the engine. Frank, his younger brother, Joe, Chet, and Chet's sister, Iola, piled out of the car and looked around.

The lot was in the middle of a huge, green forest of pine, maple, and oak trees on the fringe of Kendall State Park, several hours north of Bayport, the Hardys' hometown. Several dirt pathways—

some wide enough for a car—led from the parking area into the woods.

"*Warp Space* will need a big SFX budget to turn these woods into another planet," Joe Hardy said. He ran one hand through his wavy blond hair and squinted into the morning sunlight.

"*Nothing* about this show is big budget," Chet commented.

Iola crinkled her nose at her older brother. "Hey," she said, "I didn't notice you cutting down *Warp Space* when you entered me in this contest—without even asking."

"Well, it was against the rules for me to enter myself twice," Chet said, shrugging. He smiled at his younger sister. "I figured you'd give the prize to me because you wouldn't want it."

"Not want a bit part on a TV show," Iola said, her gray eyes sparkling. She shook her short dark hair and flashed her best movie-star smile. "It was *my* entry that won, even if you did fill it out. I can hardly wait to see my name up in lights."

Chet stuffed his hands into his jeans pockets, sighed, and leaned against the van. "But you've never even *watched* the show," he said.

"I've done a lot of research on the Internet since I won," Iola said, "and I watched your collection of tapes, too. I bet I know more about *Warp Space* than you do now."

"I don't think you can win this argument, Chet," Joe said.

"Tell me about it," Chet replied. "She may be your girlfriend, Joe, but I have to live with her." All four of the teens chuckled.

Frank checked his watch and frowned. "Wasn't the producer supposed to meet us now?" he asked.

"The executive producer," Chet said. "Sandy O'Sullivan."

"And head writer," Iola added. "She also created the series."

"And she does a lot of the publicity, too," Chet put in.

Frank shot a look at his brother. "I feel like I'm in an episode of *Can You Top This*?" he said.

"Just a little of the old Morton competitiveness," Joe said, grinning at Iola. She crinkled her nose at him.

Just then a blue SUV appeared on one of the dirt trails. The car skidded to a halt in the lot, and a thin woman with close-cropped brown hair hopped out.

"Are you the Morton party?" she asked, and they all nodded. "Sorry I'm late." She walked across the dusty lot and extended her hand to Iola. "I'm Sandy O'Sullivan. You must be Iola. Congratulations on winning a week in *Warp Space*."

Iola shook hands with her. "Thanks," she said. "These are my guests. The big oaf is my brother,

Chet. The handsome blond guy is my boyfriend, Joe Hardy, and the tall, dark-haired one is his brother, Frank."

Sandy nodded at the young men. "Pleased to meet you all. We're running a bit late, so if you'll all hop into my car, we can ride out to the location."

The four teens climbed into the SUV, and Sandy took the wheel. "Behind schedule is *Warp Space*'s natural state of being," she said. "Producing a science-fiction series is always tricky. Fasten your seat belts."

"Atomic batteries to power; turbines to speed," Joe whispered as he and the others buckled in.

Sandy hit the accelerator, and the SUV tore down the dirt road back into the forest.

"Why did you choose Kendall State Park for this shoot?" Frank asked.

"The park is fairly close to our production headquarters in Jewel Ridge," Sandy said. "Plus, it has a nice selection of natural settings to shoot in—good rocks, trees, fields, ponds, etc."

"Still pretty earthlike, though," Joe remarked.

Sandy nodded. "That's true, but I think SF fans are tired of papier-mâché sets. Shooting outdoors is tricky, but it gives a high-quality feel to the series."

"That's one of the things I like about the show," Iola said. "It doesn't look like it's all shot in a box."

"With so much programming out there," Sandy said, "we're doing everything we can to stand out."

"Fan buzz about the show is good," Chet said, "and the Web site is fabulous."

"Thanks," Sandy said. "I work on the site myself when I have time, which is not a lot lately. I've got some helpful fans working on it, too. They're out in Renton, Washington, even though we're based on the East Coast. Isn't the Internet wonderful?" She smiled again and turned the SUV down another trail. The forest gradually gave way to a grassy meadow. Huge boulders, like immense stone turtles, dotted the landscape.

"I think I've seen those boulders before," Iola said.

"Yeah," Sandy replied. "We used that location in the 'Petrified Planet' episode. The spot we're using today is just over those closest hills. The area is closed to the public just for today. I hope that's going to be enough time. If it's not, we'll have to wait until the end of the week before they can clear the area again."

"I saw on the news that the show may not be renewed because of production troubles," Frank said.

"We haven't had any more problems than most new shows," Sandy replied. "Just the usual overtime and budget woes. We've had some on-set accidents lately, but that's because everyone's nervous about renewal, and when you're nervous, you get careless." She reached into a folder on the front seat beside her and pulled out a bound script. "Here's your script, Iola," she said. "It's a bit part, so you've just got a couple of lines."

Iola took the script and glanced at it. "I'll try my best, Commander," she said, quoting Ensign Allura, one of the show's most popular characters.

Sandy laughed, as did Chet. Frank and Joe shrugged, not getting the joke.

"I'm sure you'll do great," Sandy said. "We've got a super cast. You'll meet some of them today; the rest you'll meet tomorrow. With luck, we'll get all the outdoor location shots we need today and then spend the rest of the week in Jewel Ridge doing interiors."

"Sounds good," Iola said.

They topped the next hill and drove down toward a camp of equipment trucks and production tents in the small bowl valley below. Beyond the tents lay a meadow and a small pond. Copses of trees dotted the valley and the hillside beyond. Sandy hit the brakes at the bottom of the hill and parked the SUV next to the generator truck.

As they got out, they noticed an attractive woman in a red Spacefleet uniform walking toward them. "Glad you're back," she called to Sandy. "Webb's about to blow a gasket. There was some kind of trouble with Peck's Slayer from Sirius costume, and then a stand of lights blew. We really need to get hopping if we're going to finish up today."

Sandy rubbed her forehead. "Yow! And it's not even nine A.M. yet!"

The woman in the red jumpsuit propped her hands on her hips. "In Spacefleet we do more by ten A.M. than most people do all day," she said mock seriously. "Is this the contest winner?"

"You're Commander Indira!" Iola said. "I'm so happy to meet you! I'm Iola Morton, the contest winner. This is my brother, Chet, and my friends Joe and Frank Hardy."

"Claudia Rajiv," the woman in red said, shaking hands with Iola. "Call me Claudia. Commander Indira is just the character I play."

Iola blushed. "I'm sorry," she said. "I know that, it's just—well, I'm used to watching you on TV."

Claudia laughed. "I get that all the time. Pleased to meet you all."

"Pleased to meet you," Joe and Frank echoed.

"I'm a big fan of yours," said Chet, shaking the actress's hand.

Claudia took in Chet's tall, stocky physique. Her eyes sparkled with laughter, but she didn't utter a sound.

"Chet always leaves himself open like that," Joe said. "It's one of his more endearing qualities."

"I'm sure he has many," Claudia said. "I need to get back in front of the camera. I'll see you all later."

"The rest of you, follow me," Sandy said, leading

7

them through the small tent-city set up beyond the trucks. "We have to get Iola to makeup."

They made their way to a pavilion near the center of camp. "The makeup and effects tent," Sandy explained. "Even in the wilderness, our stars need to look good."

As they approached the tent, a stocky man in armor came out between the flaps. Under his arm, he carried a domed black helmet with a narrow eye slit.

"The Slayer from Sirius!" Chet blurted. "Cool!"

"That's Peck Wilson," Sandy said. "He's the stunt-man under most of our monster costumes."

"Hey, Sandy, you're just in time," Wilson said. "Pekar's finished with me and ready for the contest winner."

"Great," Sandy said. "This is Iola, our winner, her brother, Chet, and her friends Joe and Frank."

"Pleased to meet you," Peck Wilson said. "I'm going to pop over the ridge and have a smoke." He hooked his thumb toward a small hill nearby. "Send for me when Webb's ready."

"Okay," Sandy said as Wilson walked off.

"Why is he going that far away?" Joe asked.

"Webb's a health nut," Sandy said. "Hates smoke." She pulled back the flap of the big tent and ushered the teens in. Inside, a man with a bushy beard and long, graying hair was cleaning up around one of the three makeup chairs. "Stan Pekar, our makeup and effects man," Sandy said. She introduced the teens to Pekar.

"Pleased to meet you," Pekar said, not looking up from his work as he pulled out new brushes, some paint, and a latex nose appliance. He put the new equipment in a small tray and walked over to Iola, checking her face from every angle. "Hey, we got lucky," he said, smiling. "I can work with this. Great. Take a seat, will you? This shouldn't take more than an hour."

Iola sat down. Pekar draped a makeup bib around her and began to work. "You're going to be an Alturan in this scene," Pekar said. "You know what that is?"

"Sure," Iola said.

"Try not to talk," Pekar said. "It's harder to work when you talk. And don't move your head, either."

"Mmm-hmm," Iola said.

Sandy whispered to the others. "Stan's eccentric, but he's brilliant. We were lucky to lure him out of retirement to do this show."

The three young men nodded. "I've heard of Stan Pekar," Frank said, "and I'm not even a big SF fan."

Just then a tall woman with long, braided blond hair and pointed ears walked into the tent. She was dressed in a blue Spacefleet jumpsuit and high heels. She moved gracefully despite the rough ground inside the tent.

"Sandy, thank heaven I found you," she said. "Webb wants my character to run downhill—in these heels, if you can believe it. I'm happy to do my part, but I'm not willing to break my neck. Maybe you could rewrite the scene somehow so I arrive by shuttle or something."

"Iola, Chet, Frank, Joe," Sandy said, "meet Jerri Bell—also known as Ensign Allura. Jerri, this is our contest winner."

"Great," Bell said. "Pleased to meet you. Now, about that scene . . ."

"I'll see what I can do," Sandy said, escorting Bell toward the tent flaps. At the exit Sandy paused, turned back to the teens, and said, "I have to take care of this. You can look around the camp, if you want. Try not to break anything expensive." She gave a half smile and left.

"Actors!" Pekar huffed good-naturedly. "They're even more trouble than directors." He puttered in his toolbox and began to put on Iola's alien nose. "You can watch me work, if you like," he said. "Just stay out from underfoot."

"I think we'll catch some fresh air," Joe said. He, Chet, and Frank left the tent and looked around. Cameras and lights were set up beside the pond. A rail-thin man with sunglasses and a baseball cap was pacing behind the equipment, shouting orders to Claudia Rajiv as she walked toward the cameras.

"That's Rod Webb, the director," Chet said. "He's

terrific, a real big-market talent on a small-market budget."

As they watched, Rajiv finished her shot and walked over to Webb. The two conversed a few moments, then Webb glanced around, as if looking for someone. Spotting the teens, the director jogged toward them, concern on his tan face. He was a tall man with a graying beard and mustache. His Red Sox cap held his shaggy hair in place, and a pair of black-rimmed glasses perched on his nose.

"Are you the contest winner?" the director asked Chet breathlessly. "Why aren't you in costume? We've got to get rolling here!"

"My sister won the contest," Chet said. "She's in makeup."

"Terrific," Webb said, meaning just the opposite. He glanced around and sniffed the air. "Is one of you smoking? There's no smoking on the set."

"Not us," Joe said. "We're tobacco free. But that slayer guy . . ."

"Wait a minute, Joe," Frank said. "I smell it, too, and it's not cigarettes."

From behind the hill beyond camp, black smoke billowed into the morning sky. Then small tongues of orange flame danced atop the nearby ridge.

Chet gasped. "Fire!"

2 Lights . . . Camera . . . Fire!

"Do you have fire extinguishers?" Joe asked Webb.

"Four, I think, in the electrical and generator truck," Webb said.

"We'll do what we can," Frank said. "Chet, find a phone and call the park rangers. Mr. Webb, get your crew and start hauling water from the pond."

The director was too surprised to say anything except "Right." He ran off, shouting directions. Cast and crew members rushed out of tents to assist in fighting the fire.

Chet ran for a cell phone, while Joe and Frank found the electrical truck and hauled out the heavy metal fire extinguishers. They hauled the extinguishers to the ridge.

"It could be worse," Joe said, blinking back the

smoke. He sprayed one extinguisher at the base of the flames.

Frank dropped his extra extinguisher and did the same. "I think we can keep it at bay," he said. "Good thing there's been rain here recently."

"Yeah," Joe said. "I wouldn't want to try this with a California brushfire."

The wind shifted, and despite their efforts the fire began to skirt their defensive line. Frank coughed the smoke out of his lungs. "We need help," he said. "Where are Webb and his crew?"

Joe glanced back downhill. "They're coming. But they look pretty disorganized."

"Good thing I'm here, then," Chet said, loping uphill. He took Joe's extra extinguisher and joined the brothers in battling the blaze. "I called the rangers," he said.

Together the three friends curbed the blaze's flanking maneuver and began to push the fire back uphill. As they did, the crew from *Warp Space* arrived, hauling buckets of water and soaked blankets. Iola, partially made-up as an alien, ran up and threw a bucket of water on the fire. "Are you all right?" she asked.

"We're fine," Joe replied.

"How did this happen?" Sandy O'Sullivan called as she beat at a nearby patch of flames with a wet blanket.

"Maybe someone dropped a match," Jerri Bell

13

suggested. She picked up the fourth extinguisher and began to spray it, inexpertly, at the flames.

"Everybody pitch in!" Webb yelled. "We need to put this fire out and get back to work! We're behind schedule as it is!" He tossed a bucket of water on the fire and headed downhill to where a ragtag bucket brigade had formed from the pond up the hill. "Where are those rangers?"

Claudia Rajiv looked around, worried. "Never mind that," she said. "Where's Peck?"

Frank and Joe shot each other a worried glance.

"He went over the hill for a smoke," Chet said.

"Frank and I will go after him," Joe said. He handed his big extinguisher to Iola. "Take this," he said. "We can make do with the one Frank has and the one that Ms. Bell is using."

Jerri handed the canister to Joe. "You might as well take it, for all the good *I'm* doing," she said. "I'm an actress, not a firefighter!"

"Shouldn't we wait for the rangers?" Sandy O'Sullivan asked.

"No time," Frank said. "Don't worry. Joe and I have had rescue training."

"Just keep the fire from spreading or flashing back on us," Joe added.

"Right," Chet said. "Be careful."

Iola handed the Hardys a bucket of water, and they doused themselves with it. They also soaked their handkerchiefs and tied them around their faces to mask out some of the smoke.

Choosing a spot where the fire had exhausted most of its fuel, they picked a path through the blaze, using their extinguishers to clear the way. They went over the top and down the far side of the hill. The wind picked up and whipped up the smoke and dust, making it difficult to see.

"Let's check that outcropping of boulders at the bottom of the hill," Joe said.

Frank nodded. "Good place to take cover," he said. "So that's a good place to start."

Cautiously, the brothers made their way toward the boulders. As they approached, they spotted a pair of alien boots sticking out from behind the rocks.

Sprinting the last few yards, Frank found Peck Wilson lying on the ground, unconscious. He knelt at Wilson's side and felt for a pulse. "He's alive," Frank said, "but he's inhaled smoke. He's scorched on the right side of his face. Plus he's got a nasty bruise on his neck—probably from keeling over. I think he'll be okay though. Too bad that costume he's wearing isn't a real space suit. He'd have been better off."

"Should we move him?" Joe asked.

Frank shook his head. "Probably not. I think I hear sirens. Let's just make sure he's comfortable and wait for the pros."

"Check," Joe said. He took off his shirt and put it under Wilson's head to serve as a pillow. "Good thing there isn't much to burn near these boulders."

"There's enough to start a fire, apparently," Frank said, "if you're careless."

"You think that's what happened?" Joe asked.

"Judging from the burn patterns, the fire looks like it spread uphill from here," Frank replied. "And there's a cigarette butt in that scorched patch just behind that boulder."

Joe kneeled down and picked up a piece of paper at the edge of the scorched area. The paper had been partially burned, but Joe could still make out the words on it. "This looks like part of a *Warp Space* script," he said.

"Probably the part Wilson was studying," Frank said.

"So, you think he was having a smoke, tossed the butt in the wrong place, and—whoosh!"

"That's how it looks," Frank said.

As they talked, the smoke from the fire started to die away. The sound of firefighters working to wrestle the blaze under control echoed over the hill to Frank and Joe. "Is anyone down there?" a deep voice called through the smoke.

"Yeah, we're here," Joe called back. "We're okay. We found the missing actor. He's unconscious and needs medical attention."

A ranger, wearing a smoke hood and carrying a fire extinguisher, appeared through the dust and smoke. He checked out Peck Wilson and made a quick call for assistance on his radio unit. "Fire's under control," he said. "You people did a good job of containing it."

"Thanks," Frank said.

"But," the ranger continued, "hiking into the smoke was a foolish thing to do. Next time, leave the fire and rescue business to the professionals."

Joe grinned amiably. "Hey, danger *is* our business."

Half an hour later Peck Wilson was packed into the back of Sandy O'Sullivan's SUV, heading for the local hospital. Rich Millani, the show's lighting man and property master, drove so that O'Sullivan could stay and do damage control at the site. Stan Pekar had taken Wilson out of the slayer costume, and the big stuntman seemed to be comfortable, even though he was barely conscious. The park rangers sent one of their men, who had EMT training, along for the ride. The rest stayed to inspect the area and make sure the fire wouldn't spring up again.

The cast and crew of *Warp Space*, including the Hardys and the Mortons, huddled near the cameras by the pond. Sandy O'Sullivan watched anxiously as the rangers combed the scorched hillside.

"I'm really worried," she said to no one in particular, "that they may decide to shut us down while they investigate the fire."

Rod Webb nodded. The director looked even

more concerned than O'Sullivan. "We can't afford to lose a whole day," he said. "We're behind schedule and over budget as it is. Who's ready to shoot?"

He and O'Sullivan took in the dirty, smudged faces of the assembled cast. All had helped fight the fire, but doing so had ruined their makeup and soiled their costumes.

"We are in deep trouble," O'Sullivan said quietly. "If we can't complete this footage today, we can't use the park again until the end of the week—assuming the rangers don't kick us out altogether because of the fire."

"Pekar," Webb barked, "we need someone to put in front of the cameras ASAP. What can you and Ms. Nelson give us?"

"Marge and I are special-effects and makeup artists," Stan Pekar said, "not miracle workers."

"Too bad Peck got hurt," Jerri Bell said. "He doesn't need makeup under that Slayer outfit." She wiped a smudge off one cheek with the sleeve of her Spacefleet uniform and tried to fix her hair, but it was no use.

"Hey," Webb said, "that's an idea. Who can we get into the Slayer from Sirius costume?"

A gangly young man with wiry brown hair stepped from the small crowd of people. "I can do it, Mr. Webb," he said.

Webb broke into a broad smile. "Great, Ramon, great. Let's get you suited up. If we shoot the Slayer sequences first, we'll have time to get Bell and Rajiv and that contest winner—what's her name?—cleaned up."

Stan Pekar crossed his arms over his chest. "Rod, I hate to tell you this, but there's no way Torres can play the Slayer."

"What?" said Ramon Torres, incensed. "I'm up to it. I've done plenty of stunts for the show."

"Pekar's right," Sandy O'Sullivan said. "Torres is about half Wilson's size."

"Marge and I don't have time to fit the costume to Ramon—not if you want us to work on the other actors."

"I can make it work," Torres said. "Just give me a shot."

"Chet would fit into the Slayer costume," Iola blurted out.

O'Sullivan's eyes lit up. "She's right, Rod. Her brother *would* fit the costume."

"Okay, we go with him, then," Webb said.

"But—" Torres began. O'Sullivan and Webb ignored him.

"Sandy, put together a release for this Morton guy," Webb said. "Pekar, you and Marge get him into the costume. Somebody dig up a script for him to study."

"He can have mine," Claudia Rajiv said. "I've got my lines down." Jerri Bell scowled at her, but Claudia ignored her and handed the script to Chet.

"The rest of you, do what you can to fix your outfits and hair," Webb said. "I want you ready when Pekar and Nelson have time for you."

Chet looked stunned. "Hey, I'm going to be on TV," he said, awestruck.

"Don't say I never did anything for you," Iola whispered.

"Looks like your entering Iola in the contest finally paid off, Chet," Frank jibed.

"Come on, big guy," Stan Pekar said. "Let's get you into costume. Iola, you come, too. The rest of the cast knows what to do to get ready for me."

"You coming, Joe?" Iola asked.

Joe shook his head. "Frank and I are going to take a look around," he said. "Get some fresh air in our lungs. We'll see you soon."

After their friends and the other actors left, Frank took a deep breath. "Boy, Hollywood sure does move fast, even when it's located in Kendall State Park."

Joe nodded. He and Frank walked through tent alleys toward the parking area.

"They seem to operate on a shoestring," Joe said. "So, they're probably used to minor crises."

As the brothers walked between two of the production vans, a voice behind them said, "I don't know what you two think you're doing, but it's not safe for you around here."

3 Chet Morton: Slayer from Sirius

Joe and Frank spun, expecting to find a park ranger closing the location down. Instead, they saw Ramon Torres standing between them and the production tents.

"What are you talking about, Torres?" Frank said. "The park rangers haven't declared the area unsafe."

Torres scowled at the brothers. "You may think that your status as friends of the contest winner makes you special, but you're not. The *Warp Space* crew is like family. You can't just walk on to the set and pick up parts on the show. People have worked hard for those opportunities."

"Is that what this is about?" Joe asked. "Chet getting to wear the Slayer costume instead of you?"

"I've slaved behind the scenes for my shot at the big time," Torres said. "I'm not going to let anybody take that chance away from me."

"Look," Frank said patiently, "the costume clearly won't fit you. What do you want them to do, shut down production?"

Torres looked surprised; apparently he hadn't considered that possibility. He frowned. "I'm just saying that you and your buddies shouldn't try to get more than you're due. Leave the rest to the pros."

"And if we don't?" Joe asked.

"Let's just say that things can be pretty tough in show business," Torres replied.

Joe stepped forward, but Frank put a hand out to keep his brother from taking the disagreement any further. "Thanks for the advice," Frank said. "We'll keep it in mind."

"See that you do," Torres said. He turned and walked back toward the tents.

"Jerk," Joe whispered.

"He seems pretty ambitious," Frank said. "I wonder how much he'd do to get a part."

"Are you thinking that he might have set that fire to hurt Wilson deliberately?"

"Maybe. Wilson did have that bruise on his head. Suppose he didn't get it by falling. Suppose that those accidents and setbacks I heard about on the news were more than just coincidence."

"But why would anyone do that kind of stuff?" Joe said. "If this show flies, everyone benefits."

Frank nodded. "Sure. I could be seeing conspiracies where there are none. Maybe I've just been at the detective game too long."

"We're a little young to consider retiring," Joe said with a grin.

"I know," Frank said, "but sometimes I feel like we've been chasing criminals for seventy-five years or so." Then he smiled. "Come on. Let's see how Chet and Iola are doing."

They met Chet coming out of the makeup tent. Marge Nelson, Pekar's assistant, was putting a few final touches on his costume. Suddenly she stopped and frowned.

"What's wrong?" Chet asked. "It fits okay."

"One of the insignias is missing," Ms. Nelson said. "It must have come off in the ruckus. I'll see if we've got another one. If not, we'll just have to go without it."

As Ms. Nelson was about to reenter the tent, Jerri Bell sauntered up. The young actress had changed out of her soiled costume into a clean one, removed her makeup, and fixed her hair. "Are you ready for me yet?" she asked.

"Claudia's in right now," Ms. Nelson said. "She'll be quick though, since she's a human character. I'm not sure if Stan wants you or the contest winner next."

"I should be next," Bell said. "I have more lines. We can always shoot the winner's stuff some other day."

"That's for Mr. Webb and Stan to decide," Ms. Nelson said pleasantly. She ducked inside the tent.

"I'd just like to say what an honor it is to work with you," Chet said to Jerri Bell. "I really love *Warp Space.*"

She smiled weakly at him. "I'm glad you like the show," she said. "I wish the circumstances were . . . better."

"That fire was a real setback," Frank said.

"One in a continuing string of minor annoyances," Bell replied, sighing theatrically.

"Like what?" Joe asked.

"Props breaking, little things going missing, last-minute script changes," Bell said. "All the usual problems that come with a low-budget production."

"Well, it looks great on the screen," Chet said.

"That's because everyone works so hard," said Marge Nelson, coming out of the tent once more. She affixed a small, starlike insignia to the front of Chet's costume. "You're all set," she said. "Report to Webb and get to work."

Chet put on the Slayer's bulky helmet. "Sure thing," he said, his words echoing from inside the silver fiberglass.

"I think that concealing faceplate is a distinct improvement, Chet," Joe said.

"Slay you later, Hardy," Chet replied, then turned and jogged toward the camera setup.

"Step into my parlor, Ms. Bell," Marge Nelson said. "The great Stan Pekar will see you now."

Jerri Bell rolled her eyes, and the two of them stepped inside. A moment later Claudia Rajiv stepped out. "Making yourselves useful?" she asked the Hardys.

"Only if you count putting out fires and saving lives," Frank replied.

"Thanks for that," Claudia said, "for the entire crew, I mean. Sometimes people get so busy around here that they forget the niceties."

"Rajiv," Webb called from across the camp. "Get over here! I need Commander Indira in this scene!"

Claudia shrugged. "See what I mean?" she said. "Come on. You can watch so long as you keep perfectly quiet. Iola will join us when Pekar's done with her."

The brothers walked across camp with Claudia. "What are *they* doing here?" Webb asked when he saw the Hardys.

"They're *watching*, Rod," Claudia said. "Their friend won the contest. They get to tag along."

"Well, just so long as they don't get in the way," Webb replied. "We're seriously behind, here."

"I already read them the riot act," Claudia said good-naturedly. "I think they'll behave." She winked at Frank and Joe.

"Well, okay, then," Webb said. "Let's get rolling. Places, everyone."

Webb and O'Sullivan spent a few moments rehearsing the scene with the actors, then a few more minutes checking the shots with the cameramen. Finally Webb took his position near the main camera and called, "Action!"

Chet Morton, the Slayer from Sirius, lumbered down the hill toward the unsuspecting Commander Indira. At the last moment, Indira sensed the presence of the evil alien. She spun and drew her blaster, but the Slayer slapped it from her hand. The gun flew across the clearing, landing off-camera in the first take, but just where it was supposed to land on the second take.

Indira struggled with the Slayer for several takes, until Webb was satisfied that they'd have a convincing-looking fight. As the fight stretched on, Jerri Bell joined the Hardys near the cameras. She looked stunning in costume and full alien makeup.

"Good thing Iola can't see the way you're looking at Ensign Allura," Frank whispered to Joe.

"Good thing Callie's on vacation, or she'd give you twice what Iola'd give me," Joe shot back.

"All right, cut!" Webb yelled. "I think we've got enough coverage on the struggle. Where's that contest winner? We're ready for her now."

"She's still in makeup," Jerri Bell said. "Stan decided he should do me first."

"At your suggestion, I suppose," Webb said, obviously peeved.

Bell shrugged. "I thought maybe Ensign Allura, instead of a walk-on actress, could save the commander," she said.

Sandy O'Sullivan frowned and crossed her arms over her chest. "I think it's up to Rod and me to make that kind of decision," she said.

Claudia Rajiv sighed. "Jerri," she said, "if you'll recall, the walk-on is supposed to distract the slayer only long enough for Indira to escape. The extra is gravely wounded in the exchange and clings to life for the rest of the story. Is that the part you want Allura to play in this episode?"

"Of course not," Bell said. "The autodoc on the ship could fix her up, and she could resume her normal duties after she rescues your character."

"I'll be the judge of that," O'Sullivan said. "And I say it stays the way I wrote it."

"Hold on a minute here," Webb said, scratching his beard. "Maybe Bell has a point. It could build suspense to have her character injured for most of the show."

"Then who takes the scenes she's supposed to play in the rest of the episode?" Sandy asked, annoyed.

"I told you, I recover," Bell said.

"You can't both recover *and* be critically injured to build suspense," Rajiv noted.

"Claudia's right," Sandy said. "We can't have it both ways. We could injure Allura in a future storyline if it'll make you happy, Jerri."

"I could suit up and save her," Ramon Torres said, stepping away from where he'd been working with one of the cameramen. "*I* could be critically injured."

"But you're not even made up," Bell said.

Webb waved his hands in the air to get everyone to quiet down. "Okay. Forget all this. It's too complicated, and we're wasting time. We'll go with it the way it's written. Where's that girl?"

"She's still in makeup, I think," Joe said. "I'll go get her if you want."

"Do that," Sandy said. "Why doesn't everyone take five while we find her? We've been going at it pretty hard."

"Fine, good," Webb said. "Make it ten. Everyone get something to drink. Especially you, Slayer. I don't want you collapsing from the heat. Why are you still wearing that helmet?"

Chet pulled off the fiberglass headpiece. Underneath, he was sweating profusely. "You didn't tell me to take it off," he said.

The crew laughed. "I admire your dedication," said Sandy, "but you're no good to us if you keel over."

"We've already lost one Slayer today," Webb said. "I can't afford to lose another one. Take ten, everyone! Make sure it's a short ten, though. We're losing our best light."

"Where are the drinks?" Chet asked.

"Over by the production tent," Claudia replied. "I'll show you."

"I didn't hit you too hard when I slapped that blaster out of your hand, did I?" Chet asked.

Claudia Rajiv laughed. "You did fine. Great for a first-timer. You've got some talent." She led Chet toward a tent on the other side of the pond. Jerri Bell went with them.

"Maybe you can keep playing the Slayer if Wilson needs some time to recover," Jerri said to Chet.

"Gosh. I hope he doesn't," Chet said, "but it sure would be cool to shoot some more scenes."

Joe and Frank watched their friend go. "Chet seems to fit right in with the movie star crowd," Joe said.

"Who'd have thunk it?" Frank replied. He and Joe adjourned to the makeup tent to get Iola.

Inside the tent, Stan Pekar was moving around furiously, touching up makeup and applying hair spray. Marge Nelson handed him what he needed, without Pekar even asking.

"Director Webb wants Iola on the set," Joe said.

"What am I, a miracle worker?" Pekar asked. "I have to rework the whole cast, and he wants it all done in minutes."

"She looks fine now," Ms. Nelson said. "I think

we can send her out without ruining your reputation."

"All right," Pekar said, stepping back. "You can go. Do me proud."

"I will," Iola said seriously.

Pekar and Nelson laughed. After a moment Iola and the Hardys joined in.

"Get to the set, cadet," Pekar added, saluting and clicking his heels.

"Yes, commander," Iola said, saluting back.

She turned and left the tent at a jog, with Joe and Frank trailing behind. She cut up the alley between the tents and headed for the cameras.

"She looks great in the uniform," Joe said to Frank, but Frank wasn't listening. Instead, the elder Hardy's eyes were fixed on the long electrical cable snaking across Iola's path.

"Iola, look out!" Frank called.

Too late.

Her boot caught on the cable and she tripped. She staggered, tried to right herself, and fell against the pole of a tall light stand. The light sparked, and some bulbs burst with the impact. Both Iola and the light stand slowly toppled toward the pond.

4 Downtime: Canceled

"Iola!" Joe yelled, racing toward his girlfriend.

Iola struggled as the metal of the light stand groaned, but her foot was caught in a loop of the electrical cable. She pushed away from the light tower and collapsed to the ground. "Joe!" she called.

Frank ran up behind his brother and caught the light stand just as Joe reached Iola. The older Hardy seized the metal stanchion with both hands and pulled. "I can't hold it for long!" he said.

Joe grabbed Iola under the arms and pulled her away from the light stand. The loop of cable slipped away from her ankle, and she popped free. Iola and Joe toppled backward, landing in a tangle of arms and legs.

Realizing that he couldn't keep it from collapsing, Frank let go of the lighting tower. With a loud creak and a shudder, the metal stanchion fell. Frank leaped back, and Joe and Iola stumbled away as the light standard toppled into the pond.

A resounding bang echoed through the park as the lights shorted out. A surge of power raced from the lights back to the electrical truck. Sparks flew from the control circuits, and smoke poured from the main generator.

The cast and crew of *Warp Space* poured from the tents to see what was happening. Chet, Claudia Rajiv, Jerri Bell, Sandy O'Sullivan, and director Rod Webb came running.

"What's going on?" Webb barked. "What happened to the power?"

"Iola tripped over an electrical cable, and a light stand fell into the pond," Frank said. His eyes caught someone moving away from the camp, even as the others arrived.

"Great! Just great!" Webb said. "Where's Rich Millani? He's supposed to be in charge of this stuff." The director walked to the generator truck and turned off a master control switch. The generator stopped smoking.

"Rich took Peck to the hospital, remember?" Sandy said. She took a small extinguisher from the cab of the truck and sprayed the generator.

"Wonderful!" Webb said. "That means we have no chance of getting this fixed today."

"I could take a poke at it, chief," Stan Pekar offered.

Webb shook his head. "No. No way. Then we'd have trouble with both our insurance *and* the union. We have enough problems as it is. That's a wrap, people. We'll have to pick this up at the end of the week."

"But that'll set us back on both our schedule and our budget," Sandy said. "It might even require overtime."

"I don't know what to tell you," Webb replied. "This kind of thing happens when you're working with amateurs."

"That's not really fair," Claudia Rajiv said. "Any one of us could have tripped over that cable."

"The cable wasn't there earlier," Frank said. "It must have gotten moved during the commotion over the fire."

"Well, it doesn't matter how it got moved," Webb said. "We don't have power to continue the shoot today. Everybody pack up your gear. We're heading back to Jewel Ridge."

"Just another day in *Warp Space*," Stan Pekar said, shaking his head. "Come on, Marge. Let's put our gear away."

Sandy O'Sullivan appeared crestfallen. "Everybody remember to return your costumes to wardrobe and your props to Stan, since Rich isn't here." She turned to the teens. "Iola and Chet, you'd better let Stan and Marge help you out of those getups."

Iola sighed. "My first day on TV and I don't even get to shoot a scene," she said.

"Don't worry," Sandy said. "We'll work you in somewhere else. It may not be as glamorous a part as being wounded by the Slayer from Sirius, but—"

"Oh, I wasn't complaining," Iola said. "It's been thrilling, even if I didn't get on camera."

"A little too thrilling, I'd say," Jerri Bell said.

"Come on, Jerri," Claudia Rajiv said. "We need to get out of costume, or we'll have fans following us home." Jerri nodded and the two of them headed for the costume tent. Chet and Iola walked to the makeup tent to get their gear removed.

"Oh, my gosh!" Sandy said as they left. "Rich still has my car! I need to find a ride home."

"We'd be happy to give you a lift," Frank said, "if someone can ferry us to the parking lot."

"I'm sure I can arrange that," Sandy said. "Thanks, guys."

"No trouble," Joe said. "We need someone to show us the way to our hotel, anyway."

At that moment a ranger who had been patrolling the scorched area came down into the camp. "What's all the commotion?" he asked.

"An accident with the electrical truck," Sandy said. "We're quitting for the day. We'll be back at the end of the week, though, with any luck."

"The fire's out," the ranger said, "but we'd appreciate it if you'd be more careful in the future. The guy in the hospital must have been careless with his cigarette."

"Peck's usually very conscientious," Sandy said.

"Nevertheless. Our people will probably want to talk with your lawyers about it."

Sandy sighed. "All right. You have the number in the location use contract that we signed."

The ranger nodded. "Right. Is there anything we can do to help you get going?"

"Well, some of us need a lift back to the main parking lot," Joe said.

"I'll send someone down with a truck," the ranger replied. Nodding goodbye, he hiked back over the ridge.

"I need to organize a few things before I can leave," Sandy said. "I'll meet you back here after Chet and Iola are out of costume."

"Sounds good," said Frank.

Some of the tents were already coming down as Sandy hiked off. The Hardys paced around the area, watching the commotion.

"Do you think TV shows are always this exciting?" Joe asked.

"I doubt it," Frank replied. "I'm sure that cable

wasn't there earlier. That and the fire make two accidents in one day."

"It could just be the hustle and bustle of the production," Joe said. "Everybody seems on edge, and we know they're short on both time and money."

"Could be," Frank said. "But, after the lights fell, when everyone was coming to see what happened, I saw someone taking off into the hills away from camp."

"A ranger, maybe?" Joe suggested.

Frank shrugged. "Let's just stay on our toes," he said.

"So, where are we staying?" Joe asked as he pulled the van onto the highway.

"The Benson studio in Jewel Ridge," Sandy said.

"The studio?" Iola said.

"We're giving you the guest star trailer on the lot," Sandy said. "It's a nice touch, don't you think?"

"Cool," Chet said.

"And saves money, too, I'll bet," Frank added.

Sandy grinned sheepishly. "Busted."

"Did you hear anything more about Mr. Wilson?" Iola asked.

"Rich called my cell phone and said that Peck was okay, but he'll miss a couple of days of shooting," Sandy said. "It looks like we'll be needing Chet for a while longer."

"Cool," Chet said again. "Not that I'm glad that

Mr. Wilson's hurt. I hope he recovers real soon."

"Well, until he does, you've got a job," Sandy said. "Unless, of course, Rod Webb objects."

"He seems pretty high strung," Joe said.

"He's got a lot riding on this," Sandy said. "He's not getting his usual fee, just a percentage—and a chance to finish his last contractual obligation with UAN. If the show's a big hit, he'll do well, if not . . . well, let's just say that the bread lines are long in showbiz. It's the same for most everyone on *Warp Space*, including me. We've come a long way in a very short time, and there's a lot at stake."

Joe nodded. "WUAN has gone from a local superstation to the United America Network in just a year."

"Despite our original programming, we're still just an upstart," Sandy said. "We've got a long way to go to compete with the big networks."

"But *Warp Space* is a good start," Chet said.

"Assuming UAN gives the show time to grow," Sandy replied.

"Are you worried about cancellation?" Iola asked.

"A new show, like ours, is *always* in danger of cancellation," Sandy said. "Especially if the show is different from the norm."

"Even small networks are quick to pull the plug on unprofitable programs," Frank said.

"Funding for new shows is in short supply,"

Sandy said. "So we're trying to maximize our yield in story, production, and advertising."

"Thus, the great Web site," Iola said.

"And the contest we . . . Iola won," Chet put in.

The whole group laughed. "It's okay for you to feel like a winner, too, Chet," Iola said. "However, I'll be really upset if I don't get at least *some* screen time."

"Don't worry," Sandy said. "I guarantee we'll get you into the show."

"I'm already having a great time," Chet said. "Despite everything."

Iola rolled her eyes. "Fire, flood, earthquake . . . my brother could have fun in any disaster."

Sandy said, "I hope we've had our share of bad breaks for this episode. With any luck, it should be smooth sailing from here on out."

A few hours later, Joe pulled the van off the highway into Jewel Ridge. The city was once a factory town, but it had ridden the high-tech boom back to prosperity. Expensive new housing had replaced the factories that once lined the city's central river.

Following Sandy O'Sullivan's directions, Joe wound through the New England streets to the Benson lot. The studio was in one of the less prosperous sections of town, surrounded by empty warehouses and a few old factories.

"Not quite Hollywood, is it?" Sandy said wistfully as they pulled up to the studio gates.

"How old is this studio?" Frank said.

"It was founded in the twenties by movie-serial pioneer Gus Benson," Sandy replied. "The studio did pretty good business before shutting down in the fifties. Scott Broadcasting did some rehab work on it in the seventies. It's been functioning on and off since then. UAN snapped it up when they needed a cheap production facility."

"I think it has character," Iola said.

They pulled up to the gate, and a sleepy-looking guard waved them through. The studio had a number of large, warehouselike buildings, a smattering of trailers—some for stars, others serving as offices—a security office, and a cafeteria with vending machines and storage lockers outside. The biggest of the warehouses had a fancy sign on the outside, which read, *Warp Space*—Studio One.

"You don't have to be a detective to figure out where the show is shot," Frank said.

"Are all of these big buildings stages?" Iola asked.

"No," Sandy said. "A lot of them are taken up with storage. One has Stan Pekar's workshop in it. The UAN execs have some offices on the far end of the lot." She smiled. "They have a fancier parking lot and a better view.

"You, on the other hand," she continued, "have a great view of the soundstage, and the offices of the *Warp Space* production crew. At least you don't have far to walk to get to work in the morning."

"What's the building over there with the light on?" Chet asked.

"Those self-same offices. Rod Webb and I have space on the side nearest your trailer. The part abutting the soundstage is where Stan Pekar works his magic. You'll probably be going there first thing in the morning. Makeup call is at four A.M., so you'll want to get a good night's rest."

"Sounds fine by me," Iola said. "I just want to have some dinner and crash."

"Will you join us, Sandy?" Frank asked.

She sighed. "I wish I could, but I'm afraid I have to spend some time pulling the shooting schedule back together. I'll have a cab take you to a great pizza place I know—on the studio, of course."

"Maybe we could bring you something back," Chet suggested.

"No," Sandy said. "I'll be working at home. Thanks for offering, though. Just make sure you're ready for shooting bright and early."

"We will be," Iola and Chet said simultaneously.

The teens dumped their bags in the trailer. Then they all went out for dinner. After a good meal at the Town Spa pizza parlor, they went back to their trailer for the night. Before Sandy had taken a cab home, she had given them gate passes, which got the four friends past the guard. He waved the teens through and welcomed them to the *Warp Space* family.

"That was so cool!" Chet said.

"I really feel like a star," Iola added.

"Just wait until you get in front of the cameras," Joe said, smiling.

Frank used the keys to open the trailer, and they all piled into the small, streamlined space. The inside was a bit cramped, but well kept and cleverly arranged. There were two small bedrooms and a private bath, as well as a dining area with a tiny kitchen and a refrigerator.

As Chet scoped out the fridge, Iola went to get ready for bed. "I can't believe you're hungry," she called to her brother. "We just ate!"

"I'm just seeing what's available," Chet said.

"One never knows when the urge for a midnight snack might strike," Joe commented.

"Men!" Iola said. She went into one of the bedrooms and shut the door. A moment later she reappeared, dressed in the same clothes but looking pale and shaken. "I think you should see this," she said.

The Hardys and Chet scrambled through the narrow door into the bedroom.

Iola's pillow had been slashed. A dark red stain spread out over the torn cloth, and in the middle of the stain lay a smashed figurine of the Slayer from Sirius.

5 Sirius Business

"D-Do you think that's blood?" Iola asked. Joe put an arm around her and gave her a reassuring hug.

Frank leaned close to the pillow and shook his head. "It smells like ketchup to me," he said.

"There's a half-empty bottle of ketchup in the fridge," Chet suggested.

Joe scowled. "Who could have done this, and why?"

"And why did they single *me* out?" asked Iola.

"I wouldn't be sure that whoever did this intended it for you, Iola," Frank said.

"Maybe it's just a prank," Chet said, "a joke on the new kids."

"If it's a prank, it's not funny," Joe said angrily.

"It's not," Frank said. "But it's possible that Chet could be right."

"Frank, if you're trying to spare my feelings, I wish you wouldn't," Iola said.

"I'm going easy on you," Frank said, "it's just that we don't have much to go on here. We've got a slashed pillow stained with ketchup and a broken statuette in our trailer. Clearly, it's a staged event, but the ketchup makes it seem like a spur-of-the-moment act."

"The smashed figure makes it look premeditated to me," Joe said.

"I've seen some of these figurines for sale on the Internet," Chet said. "The show doesn't have a big toy deal yet, but they made a few for publicity. They're pretty valuable."

"I saw one go for a hundred dollars on VBuy," Iola added.

"So, breaking one deliberately is like throwing money away," Frank said.

"Unless it was already broken," Joe said, "and someone was just looking for a good 'use' for it."

"From what I remember reading, the figures were mostly given to the cast and crew," Iola said.

"That would fit in with it showing up here," Frank said.

"And only a few people know we're on the lot and staying in this trailer," Joe said. "Probably the person behind this is someone we've met, someone with access to the lot—one of the cast or crew."

"Some fans know everything about the show, including when the prize was supposed to be awarded," Chet said. "A jealous contest loser might be behind this, too."

"Could be," Joe said. "The question remains, though, is this a prank, a threat against Iola or Chet—he was the one in the Slayer costume today—or is it some kind of mischief against the show in general?"

"This is the first thing we've seen that couldn't be just bad luck or a mistake," Frank said. "I'm not a big believer in coincidence, though."

"Me neither," Chet said. "The incidents sure are piling up."

"But why would anyone want to frighten *us?*" Iola asked.

Joe shrugged. "I'm going outside to have a look around."

"I'll go with you," Iola added.

"Good idea," Frank said. "We'll check the trailer for clues."

Joe and Iola walked around the trailer and the surrounding area while Frank and Chet searched inside. Joe and Iola looked for suspicious characters, talked with security guards, and looked into trash cans. After half an hour Joe and his girlfriend returned.

"The figurine and the ketchup bottle are the only clues we could find in the trailer," Frank said.

"We talked to a few security guards," Joe said. "They said most of the show's cast had been in and out this evening, which leaves us a very broad suspect list."

"I found a packing knife in a trash can near the cafeteria," Iola said, holding out a small, yellow-handled knife. "Maybe it was used to slash the pillow."

Frank sighed and shook his head. "Maybe, but it could just be one from a studio worker. Short of fingerprinting the cast, we've hit a dead end."

"I think Ramon Torres did this," Chet said. "He seemed pretty ticked when I got to play the Slayer from Sirius."

"But he's had a number of parts on the show," Iola said. "Why would losing this one upset him so much?"

"Maybe he saw it as his big break," Chet suggested. "The Slayer is a very popular character."

"For an alien whose face is never seen," Joe added.

"It's pointless to speculate without more information," Frank said. "Let's turn in. You Mortons have an early call tomorrow."

"I don't know if I *can* sleep after all this," Iola said.

"Just think of your brother's snoring as a lullaby," Joe said, grinning.

45

"Big help you are, Joe Hardy!" Iola said, shutting the door to her bedroom.

It seemed only moments later that someone was pounding on their door.

"Makeup call!" Marge Nelson called from outside. "Roll out and hit the chairs!"

"Four A.M. already?" Chet groaned. He staggered to his feet and opened the small bedroom door.

"Shake a leg, big brother," Iola said. She stepped out of the bathroom fully dressed and drying her hair with a towel.

"Ugh," Joe said, sitting up. "How can you be so awake this early?"

Iola shrugged cheerfully. "I told you I probably wouldn't sleep very much. So, I decided to put my time to good use. Are you boys going to sleep in or get up?"

"I think better on a full night's rest," Frank said groggily. He didn't even lift his head from the floor of the bedroom he was sharing with Joe and Chet.

"Are you alive in there?" Ms. Nelson called, still banging on the door.

"We're coming," Iola called back to her. "I'll be out in a minute."

"Well, hustle over to the makeup room as fast as you can," Ms. Nelson said. "You know where it is, right?"

"Sure," Iola replied. "We'll be there at warp speed."

"What do you mean, 'we,' Spacefleet scum," Chet grumbled.

Iola propped her hands on her hips. "Honestly, you Slayers from Sirius are such babies!"

A little more than two hours later the Hardys rolled into the makeup studio. Stan Pekar, Marge Nelson, and two other assistants were hard at work on the actors needed for the day's shoot, a cast that included Jerri Bell as well as Chet and Iola.

Ms. Nelson had just finished with Iola as they arrived. She dusted off Iola's costume one final time before going to work on Chet's Slayer outfit. Sandy O'Sullivan was hovering nearby with a stack of papers in her hand. She looked tired and nervous.

Joe and Frank walked over to Iola. "You look different today," Joe said. Iola sported a golden uniform, and her alien makeup had changed.

"My idea," Sandy said. "We wanted to get Iola finished today, so we changed her part. That way, she can get the acting part of her prize over and get on with enjoying the shoot." Sandy handed some of the pages she was holding to Iola. "Sorry, there aren't a lot of lines, but I'm sure you'll be wonderful."

"Thanks," Iola said. "I'll do my best."

"The great thing about my part," Chet called from across the room, "is that there are no lines."

"Keep still," Ms. Nelson cautioned. "We need to make sure the suit matches the shots from yesterday."

"You look pretty nervous," Frank said to Sandy. "Is anything wrong?"

"Just tired," Sandy said. "I was up late working on the rewrites. The studio accountants are breathing down my neck, too." She managed a smile. "Don't worry, though. I can handle it."

"Who's getting Iola's old part?" Joe asked.

"Ramon Torres," Sandy said. "But do you think he's grateful?" She shook her head and turned to Iola. "Come on, we've got to get you to the set. Frank and Joe, follow us. We don't need extra people hanging around makeup." As they left the building she added in a whisper, "Especially when Stan's working on Jerri. Both of them are *very* particular."

They walked the short distance from the makeup studio to the main production stage. Sandy smiled at Iola and the Hardys. "Get ready," she said, "to enter Wonderland."

She opened a heavy door onto the vast soundstage. Inside, the teens recognized the interior set of the *Warp Space* starship. Stagehands, grips, and gaffers bustled around, getting the sets ready for the day's work.

"The engine room!" Iola said, her eyes lighting up.

"And just over there is the bridge," Sandy said, pointing to the left. "And behind the engine room, the infirmary, the shuttle bay, and a lot of other places you'll recognize, too."

"What set am I working on today?" Iola asked, flipping through her pages, trying to find her scene.

"The briefing room," Sandy said. "You'll be working with Claudia and Bruce Reid."

"Captain Winter himself?" Iola said, beaming.

Sandy smiled. "Yes, I— Oh, no! I forgot to get Bruce today's pages!" She looked around, almost frantically. "Here comes Claudia, ask her to help you out. I've got to run!" With that, Sandy dashed out the way they'd come.

Claudia Rajiv, dressed in her Commander Indira costume, walked over to the group. She seemed calm and ready to work. "Where's Sandy going?" she asked.

"She forgot to give Captain Winter his pages," Joe said. "She said you'd help us get set up."

Rajiv laughed. "It's always something around here. Follow me. I'll give you the nickel tour. They don't need us on the set for another half hour. If we got there now, Rich Millani would just yell at us. He's fixing something with the electricals."

As Claudia gave them a quick tour, the Hardys and Iola were impressed with the level of detail on the sets.

"I could almost believe I'm in the twenty-third century," Joe said.

"Rich Millani and Stan Pekar have worked hard

on the physical effects," Claudia Rajiv said. "Imagine what they could do if we had a real budget."

Everywhere they went, stagehands bustled to and fro. They ran into Ramon Torres near the ship's infirmary, but he pointedly ignored them. Rod Webb was pacing like a caged tiger, growling at anyone who got too close.

As they arrived back at the briefing room set, Rich Millani crawled out from under a control panel and dusted himself off. "I swear," he said, "we have gremlins on this stage. The rate these wires wear out!"

"Maybe it's rats," Rajiv said. "This place is old enough."

Iola made a disgusted expression. "Eew!" she said. "Please leave me my futuristic illusions!" All of them laughed, and then Millani scurried off to his next job.

Sandy returned to the set, walking behind a distinguished-looking older man with short dark hair and graying temples. "I am so sorry, Bruce," she said. "I meant to have the pages to you earlier, but, well . . . you know how things get around here."

"Honestly, it's all right," Bruce Reid said. "No need to keep apologizing. I've been at this a long time. A few new lines aren't going to throw me off my game."

"Bruce, you are almost too good to be true," Rajiv called to him.

"So are you, Claudia," he called back. "Who are the civilians?"

"This lovely alien creature is our contest winner, Iola Morton," Rajiv said. "And these are her friends Frank and Joe Hardy. Her brother is around somewhere, too. He's filling in for Peck."

"Chet's in makeup," Iola said.

Bruce Reid broke into a million-dollar smile. "Pleased to meet you all," he said. "I hope you'll have a great visit with us here in *Warp Space*." He shook hands with both the Hardys then took Iola's hand and kissed it, causing her to blush.

"That's our, Bruce," Rajiv said. "A lady-killer on any planet."

Just then Rod Webb bustled onto the set, a sheaf of papers in one hand and a megaphone in the other. "Quiet on the set!" he called. "Places, everyone! We've got a lot of work to do today. Let's get down to business."

"Keep well behind the lights," Sandy whispered to the Hardys. "Stay out of Rod's sight while he's working, and don't talk when the cameras are rolling." She paused, and a flash of panic washed over her features. She slapped her forehead. "Oh, no! I still have Geoff's pages, too! Where is my brain today?" Raising her voice she called, "Rod, I'll be right back!"

"Take your time," Webb said. "We've got plenty to keep us busy."

Sandy hurried off again, and the Hardys retreated

51

as the big lights surrounding the set snapped on.

Webb worked quickly and efficiently with the actors. Iola completed her briefing room sequence with Captain Winter, then got to do a walk-by in a corridor scene between Winter and Ensign Allura. The crew moved the cameras from one set to the next as they completed each scene.

Chet, partially costumed, popped in several times during the shooting, but he never stayed long. "They keep postponing finishing my makeup," he explained. "I guess they've got other scenes to complete before mine."

"So, what are you going to do?" Frank asked.

"Tour the sets, visit the cafeteria," Chet said.

"I'll join you," Frank said. "Coming, Joe?"

The younger Hardy shook his head. "I'll wait and 'do lunch' with Iola," he replied.

When Frank and Chet got back, Iola and the others were still working. Chet went back to makeup and Frank rejoined his brother, watching the shoot.

The cast and crew only stopped for lunch.

They'd just finished setting up a shot in the ship's shuttle bay, when Chet arrived in full makeup with script in hand.

"It took you long enough," Iola whispered. "You missed all my scenes."

"Hey, it's not my fault I kept getting bumped," Chet said. "I poked my head in when Pekar wasn't strapping me into this suit. Hey, I even signed a few autographs for a tour group."

The director spotted Chet and said, "Ah! Our man from Sirius is here, just in time. Now we can finally get down to business. Do you have your lines memorized?" Before Chet could answer, Webb continued joking. "What? You have no lines? We're all set then! Put on your helmet and find your mark."

"Right, chief," Chet said, and donned the Slayer's helmet.

As he did so, a tall, buff man in a blue uniform pushed his way past the cameras. "Sorry I'm late," the man said, "but Sandy didn't get my pages to me until fifteen minutes ago."

Chet looked around to see who was talking, but the Slayer helmet obscured his view. As he turned, he nearly tripped the newcomer.

"Watch where you're going, extra!" the man said. He shoved Chet aside and walked on to the set. "Where do you want me?" he asked.

"Just outside the hangar door, Geoff," Webb called. The director was perched atop a crane to get a high-angle shot for the scene. "You're coming into the bay just as the Slayer sneaks off the shuttle. We'll work the rest of the characters into the scene after that."

"Check," said the muscular man with short blond hair.

"That's Geoff Gross," Iola whispered to the others. "He's the hotheaded Lieutenant Commander Ravenscroft."

"He seems pretty hotheaded in real life, too," Joe whispered back.

"Quiet on the set!" Webb called. "Places, everyone! Roll cameras! Action!"

In the first take, Chet stalked out of the hijacked shuttle. They did a close-up of the Slayer, then they shot Lieutenant Commander Ravenscroft entering the bay.

"Great Bird of the Galaxy!" Ravenscroft exclaimed upon seeing the Slayer. He ran forward to engage the enemy. Chet drew the Slayer's ray blaster and pointed it at the Spacefleet officer.

Ravenscroft charged, but Chet threw him aside. The Slayer pointed the gun at the fallen commander and pulled the trigger.

Sparks flew from the blaster, and smoke shot from the weapon's sleek, futuristic barrel. Before Chet could react, the gun exploded.

6 Blaster Blastoff

Smoke and sparks enveloped Chet's hand. The muzzle of the weapon shattered, spraying the air with plastic shrapnel. A few splinters hit Geoff Gross, others bounced off Chet's helmet and costume. Chet yelped and dropped the blaster as the rest of it caught fire.

"Cut!" Webb yelled. "Cut!" A stagehand ran forward and shot a fire extinguisher at the smoking weapon. Frank and Joe grabbed a towel from the back of a chair and smothered what little remained.

Geoff Gross spun on the startled Chet. "What are you doing?" he screamed. "I could have been scarred for life! Are you stupid or what?"

"I didn't do anything," Chet protested.

Gross turned to Webb. "Amateurs are always trouble on the set!"

"Actually," Rajiv said, "he's done very well."

"His sister was terrific in her scenes this morning," Reid added.

"There's no way Chet could have caused that blaster to blow up deliberately," Frank said. "It was a freak accident, that's all."

"Why would I burn my own hand?" Chet asked, recovered enough to be angry at the accusation.

Iola looked at her brother with concern. "How bad is it?" she asked.

"Just like touching a hot stove," Chet said. "But I'll be fine."

Webb fumed. "Do I need to call the insurance company?" he asked. Then immediately answered his own question. "No? Good. We're behind enough without dragging them in. Where's Millani?"

"Right here, boss," Rich Millani said, stepping out from the shadows behind the cameras.

"What happened here?" Webb demanded.

Millani shrugged. "Beats me. Could be about anything. Stan and I have warned you and the execs about going cheap on these props," he said. "Something was bound to give, sooner or later."

"I'd say a lot of things have been 'giving' around here lately," Webb said.

"Look," Millani said angrily, "you've got only two people doing all the on-set special-effects work—a few more if you count Pekar's makeup assistants. I'm handling both the props and the electrical work with a skeleton crew. If you think you can do better, you're welcome to try. Since you started as a lowly gaffer's assistant and worked your way up through the ranks, it'll probably be a snap for you to fix this stuff. Now, if you'll excuse me, I have to work on the engine room set, or we won't have any working display panels there tomorrow." He stalked away.

Ramon Torres, who was waiting nearby to enter the scene, leaned back in his chair and put his hands behind his head. "That's the *Warp Space* spirit," he said sarcastically. "One for all—and the last one out, please shut the airlock."

At that moment Sandy O'Sullivan returned to the set. "Hey!" she snapped. "If you don't have anything useful to contribute, I'll be happy to show you the door. Everyone's working too hard to put up with your bellyaching."

Webb nodded. "What Sandy said goes double for me," he said. "Anyone who doesn't want to work— and work hard—should get out. The rest of us have jobs to do, and no time for sarcastic slackers."

Bruce Reid stepped forward. "Calm down, you two," he said to Sandy and Webb. "Everyone's been working all day. It's dinner break."

Webb paused before saying, "Yeah, dinner break. Come back prepared to work."

The cast and crew grumbled their assent. Then they took off for the commissary. As they all left, Jerri Bell sauntered in. "Are you ready for me yet?" she asked, looking amazingly fresh and ready to go.

"It's dinner break," Sandy said.

Bell checked her watch. "I was hoping to get out on time tonight."

"Well, you'll just have to choose between your social life and your job," Webb called back as he left the set.

Bell frowned. "Well, when you need me, I'll be in my trailer."

"Why not join us for dinner?" Chet suggested.

She smiled slightly. "Sorry. Maybe some other time."

"What about you, Sandy and Claudia?" Iola asked.

"Sorry," Claudia Rajiv said. "I can't. I have some calls to make."

"And I have rewrites," Sandy said. "Have a good time, though." She tucked some papers under her arm and scurried off.

After Sandy was out of earshot, Claudia said, "Jerri and I are planning to go dancing after we wrap tonight. You could come with us."

"Sounds great," Chet said.

"Don't you have an early makeup call again tomorrow?" Iola asked, looking from her brother to Claudia.

"I'm used to no sleep," Claudia said.

"How can I pass up an opportunity to go out with two starlets?" Chet asked.

The Hardys and Iola laughed.

Claudia smiled. "We'll hook up after our last shots, then," she said, and headed for her trailer.

The Hardys and the Mortons went to the commissary and found a deserted corner. Only the *Warp Space* people were left on the lot.

"Well," Frank said, sipping his chocolate shake, "another accident."

"Another accident connected to me and Iola," Chet added.

"If I didn't know better," Iola said, "I'd think someone was out to get us."

"It's not just you," Joe said. "Both director Webb and Rich Millani complained about things breaking down."

"We were really lucky my ray gun didn't hurt anyone," Chet said.

"I'm surprised there's so much tension on the set," Iola said. "I knew that work on TV was tough, but I didn't imagine all this pressure."

"I don't know," Chet said around a mouthful of burger. "I'm having fun."

"Honestly, Chet," Iola said, "you're the only person I know who could have a ray gun blow up in his hand and enjoy it."

Chet shrugged and took another bite. "I'm just easygoing, I guess."

"Well," Frank said, "easygoing or not, I think we all need to keep our eyes peeled. Chet could have been injured today, and Iola was nearly hurt yesterday."

"And Peck Wilson is still in the hospital," Joe added. "Maybe this is just normal TV chaos, but we need to stay on our toes."

They all nodded, finished their dinners, and hiked back to the set.

Rod Webb picked up the scene where they'd left off. Rich Millani had dug up another blaster and personally tested it several times to make sure nothing would go wrong. Despite the new precautions, Geoff Gross still scowled at Chet between takes.

Chet and Gross ran through the scene again, and this time it went without a hitch. The Slayer zapped Lieutenant Commander Ravenscroft, and the brave Spacefleet officer managed to escape certain death only when Ensign Allura, Commander Indira, and Captain Winter put in a timely appearance.

Knowing that discretion was the better part of valor, the Slayer escaped from the shuttle bay, jamming the door so the crew couldn't follow him. By the time the heroes got the door open, their foe had hidden himself in the bowels of the ship.

Just before eleven, Webb yelled, "That's a wrap! Good job. See you bright and early, people."

The cast and crew let out a collective sigh of

relief. Quickly, everyone packed up and headed for their respective homes. Chet, Jerri Bell, and some of the other cast members headed back to Stan Pekar's studio to have their special makeup removed.

Sandy O'Sullivan, obviously bushed and ready for bed, walked over to where Iola, the Hardys, and Claudia Rajiv were waiting for Chet. "Well, I hope you all had a good first day on the lot," she said.

"Boy, things sure went slowly," Iola said. She had gotten out of her costume and makeup while Chet was working.

"Nine pages is a lot for one day," Sandy replied, "especially when you have action scenes. Another good day tomorrow and maybe the accountants will stop breathing down our necks. In any case, I'm glad that we got your scene in, Iola. You can relax from here on out."

"I won't be able to relax until my brother has his fifteen minutes of fame," Iola said jokingly.

Sandy chuckled. "Don't worry. I'm sure Peck will be out of the hospital in the next day or two."

"He's doing better, then?" Joe asked.

"Yes, much better," Sandy said. "Good thing he's got leather lungs and an iron head, even out of costume."

"Yeah," Frank said, "he was pretty lucky, considering."

"Lucky that you two were around when he got

careless, anyway," Sandy said. "Well, I've got to run. More rewrites tonight and an early call tomorrow."

"You're working more tonight?" Iola asked.

"A writer-producer's work is never done," Sandy said. "Have a good night, and I'll see you in the morning. Good night, Claudia. Make sure you get some sleep."

"No worries, boss," Claudia said.

Sandy turned and left, quickly disappearing into the darkened soundstage. Claudia Rajiv smiled. "Let's collect our friends and hit the dance floor."

They agreed to meet at the Mortons' trailer once everyone had showered and changed. Jerri and Claudia arrived surprisingly quickly. Both women looked stunning.

"I am *so* jealous!" Iola whispered to Joe.

"No need to be," he whispered back. "You're every bit as beautiful as they are." He gave her a reassuring hug.

"So, let's hit Club 451," Claudia said.

"Um, I hate to tell you," Chet said, "but we're all underage."

"That's okay," Claudia replied. "So's Jerri. Club 451 is a restaurant that just happens to have a great dance floor."

"The food is good, too," Jerri said.

Chet smiled. "We're there!"

They convoyed to the restaurant parking lot in their respective cars. The trip took ten minutes, and Claudia had called ahead to get them a table.

"Not that we'll be sitting much," she said with a wink.

Club 451 was a combination restaurant and discotheque with a techno motif. Its patrons included the young professionals of many of Jewel Ridge's high-tech firms. The restaurant and dance floor were still crowded when the Hardys and their friends arrived.

Techno music blared over the loudspeakers, and flashing lights turned the dancers into a series of multicolored snapshots. Tables on a raised platform circled the dance floor in the middle of the restaurant. The Hardys and their friends took a table opposite the main entrance. Even before Chet had a chance to order food, Claudia and Jerri hauled him onto the dance floor.

Frank and Joe chuckled.

"If you think that's funny, Joe Hardy," Iola said, "let's see how well you rock 'n' roll." She grabbed Joe's hand, and soon the two of them were dancing amid the noise and pulsing lights.

Frank took a long, deep breath and looked around. Club 451 wasn't the kind of place he'd have chosen to relax after two difficult, puzzling days. But it seemed to be working for Chet, Iola, and the others. "Guess I'm not TV star material," Frank said to no one in particular.

His gaze shifted across the crowd of dancers to

the rows of restaurant tables beyond the sunken dance floor. People walking around the dimly lit restaurant paused to watch Claudia and Jerri. Even on the crowded dance floor, the *Warp Space* women stood out like stars in a dark sky.

Most of the club's patrons paused to watch the women only a moment or two, but one patron's gaze lingered longer. The figure caught Frank's attention when he nearly knocked over a waitress carrying a rack of trays. He was a thin wiry man, but the flashing lights and shadows effectively hid his face. At the commotion, the figure slipped back behind a decorative column at the edge of the dance floor.

Frank peered into the darkness as the figure reappeared. He couldn't make out the man's features, but he watched as he moved around the room. When Chet and the girls moved, the shadowed man moved as well. When they stopped, the man stopped. When they left the dance floor and ordered sodas at the bar, the man took up a position nearby, well out of the lights.

All of them returned to the table. Frank ordered soft drinks for Joe, Iola, and himself.

"Where'd you go?" Jerri Bell asked Frank. "We needed another dancer on the floor."

"I left my dancing shoes at home," Frank said.

"Along with his girlfriend," Chet added.

They all laughed. The waitress brought their

sodas, and Chet ordered some buffalo wings.

Jerri brushed her hair out of her eyes. "Well," she said, "after all that dancing, I need to fix my makeup."

"Me, too," Claudia agreed.

"And me," Iola said. She gave Joe a quick kiss on the cheek. "Be right back."

As the three young women headed for the lounge, Frank spotted the lurking figure still following them as they moved across the room.

Seeing the expression on his brother's face, Joe asked, "What's up?"

"Remember when I thought I saw someone sneaking away from the camp yesterday?" Frank said.

"Yeah," Joe replied.

"Well, I may not have seen anyone then," Frank said, "but at the moment I'm dead sure someone is stalking Claudia, Jerri, and Iola."

7 Lights and Shadows

Joe's face turned red with anger, but he didn't say anything. Frank indicated where to look with a slight movement of his head. Joe and Chet glanced in that direction and saw the man moving stealthily through the shadows.

Joe rose from the table, "Stay here, Chet," he said. "Frank and I will take care of this."

"No way," Chet said. "I want a piece of this guy, too."

"If we all get up at once, he may get suspicious," Frank said. "Besides, we need someone to keep an eye out for the girls."

"Yeah, okay," Chet said. "Be careful."

Joe and Frank nodded. "I'll go first," Frank said. "We'll circle around and catch this creep."

"Check," Joe said.

Frank got up, stretched, and headed for the bar. Joe and Chet kept an eye on the shadowy figure. The man remained near the women's lounge, moving only when Jerri, Claudia, and Iola came out.

"He's following them, all right," Chet said.

"Not for long," Joe replied as he rose from the table. He met Frank near the bar, and the two of them watched the figure as the girls returned to their table. "Follow my lead," Joe said. Frank nodded and the two of them wound their way through the crowded darkness toward the stalker.

"A fan, you think?" Joe whispered as they crept along.

"Or it could be an old boyfriend," Frank replied. "Or just some creep."

They had moved to within thirty feet of the stalker when Jerri Bell suddenly turned in their direction and tried to wave them back to the table. The brothers saw from the expression on Chet's face that he hadn't told the others what they were up to.

The stalker suddenly moved away from the group.

"He's onto us," Joe said. "Flank right, I'll go left."

"Check," Frank said.

He and Joe fanned out, one moving on either side of the stalker. The darkness and the flashing lights made it difficult to see, and the music made it impossible for the brothers to communicate with each other. Still, the Hardys had a lot of experience in tracking criminals.

The stalker was clever, though. He tried to put as many people between himself and the Hardys as he could. He almost gave them the slip by cutting across a corner of the crowded dance floor. Joe kept the thin man in sight, though, and Frank angled toward Joe. Both brothers and the man they were pursuing headed for the back of the disco, toward a lighted Exit sign.

Joe and Frank arrived at the sign just as the stalker slipped out the back door. The brothers sprinted down a deserted hallway, out the door, and into an alley behind the club. As the Hardys exited, they saw a thin figure running away into the darkness. The Hardys chased after him.

"Hold it, you!" Joe called. The man didn't stop.

The stalker wasn't nearly as fast as the brothers, and Frank and Joe soon closed the short distance between them. Before Frank could grab him, though, the man spun on them.

He was lean and wore baggy pants and a T-shirt with a *Warp Space* logo. He seemed to be about the same age and height as the Hardys, though not as muscular. His black, curly hair fell over his darting eyes, and he regarded them with a wild look. He held a key ring in one fist, like makeshift brass knuckles, and assumed a defensive fighting stance. In his other hand, he held a cell phone.

"I'll call the cops!" he said.

"Go ahead," Joe replied. "Then you can explain to them why you were stalking those women."

"You're crazy," the man said. "I have no idea what you're talking about."

"We saw you following Jerri Bell, Claudia Rajiv, and their friend," Frank said.

"Why would I need to stalk them?" the man said. "I see them at work every day."

Frank and Joe exchanged a puzzled glance. "Who are you?" Joe asked.

"None of your business," the man said, growing bolder. "Now, scram, or I make that call."

"Be our guest," Frank said.

Before the man could punch the number into the phone, though, the back door of the club opened and Chet and the women came through.

"Matt Stiller?" Jerri Bell said, surprised.

"You mean you really *do* know this guy?" Joe asked.

Claudia laughed. "Sure we know him," she said. "He's a coffee boy and gofer at the studio. I'm surprised you didn't see him around today."

Stiller puffed out his chest. "See?" he said. "You guys are crazy, just like I said."

"But you were stalking Jerri and Claudia," Chet said. "We saw you."

"A lot of the crew hang out here," Stiller said confidently.

"I have to admit," Jerri said, giggling, "the idea of Matt stalking us is pretty ridiculous."

"Well, he was definitely keeping an eye on you," Joe said.

"I was trying to figure out if I should come over and join your party," Stiller said. "Now I'm really glad I didn't." Turning to Claudia and Jerri, he said, "These guys are creeps. You shouldn't be hanging out with them."

Claudia Rajiv smiled indulgently. "Don't worry about us, Matt," she said. "We're all grown-up now. We can take care of ourselves."

"Well, be careful anyway," Stiller said. "I'll see you tomorrow." He stuffed his hands into his pockets and walked down the alleyway.

"Wow, *that* was strange," Iola said.

"I'm certain he was secretly watching you girls most of the time we were in the restaurant," Frank said.

"Maybe he was just working up the nerve to ask us to a dance," Jerri suggested.

"Or he could have a secret crush on Jerri," Claudia said. "Nearly everyone does."

Jerri rolled her blue eyes. "Honestly, Claudia, I almost think you're jealous."

Claudia laughed. "All right," she said, "I think we've had enough excitement for one evening. Let's pay our tab and get some rest. Makeup call is early."

* * *

Though Chet got up early, Iola and the Hardys slept in a bit, then went to the studio commissary for breakfast. As they entered, they spotted Matt Stiller leaving with a trayful of coffee cups. Stiller pointedly ignored them, and the three friends walked past him to get their meals. Iola and the brothers talked quietly over their pancakes and eggs.

Frank frowned. "Maybe I'm just being paranoid, but I still think *someone* is trying to sabotage this show."

"Ramon Torres is my prime suspect," Joe said. "He's obviously upset about the way things have gone. He thought he'd get to play the Slayer if Wilson got hurt."

"It was his bad luck that Chet fit the costume better," Iola said. "What about that Stiller guy, though? I think you were right about him stalking Claudia and Jerri."

"Yeah," Frank said. "Stiller is definitely in the running. Rich Millani is a good suspect, too. He works with the props and the electrical equipment. That gives him opportunity for both the light accident and the blaster."

"But he was at the hospital with Peck Wilson when I tripped," Iola said.

Joe leaned back and put his hands behind his head. "That's a good alibi, though he could have

71

moved the cable earlier. With the fire, everyone might have overlooked it. Or, I suppose, it could have been a normal accident." He sighed. "We'll just have to stay on our toes."

"And try to make sure no one else gets hurt," Frank said.

"Well, you can count on me," Iola said. Joe gave her a quick hug.

As they finished eating, Chet chugged in with his Slayer helmet under his arm. "Hey, guys, just picking up a soda before shooting. You wouldn't believe how hot this suit is. You want to catch my first scene of the day?"

"Wouldn't miss it," Joe said. They picked up Chet's drink, then headed for the door. Sandy O'Sullivan breezed in just as they were leaving.

"Chet," she said, smiling, "I'm so glad I caught you. Here are today's pages." She handed him a dozen or so sheets of paper. "Peck might be back as early as tomorrow, so enjoy your time in the costume."

"Loving every minute," Chet said, smiling back.

"Oh, and, Iola, if you'd like to do some more walk-throughs, let me know, and we'll have Stan suit you up in something."

"That might be fun," Iola said. "What kind of aliens do you need in upcoming scenes?"

"Walk with me and I'll fill you in," Sandy said. "I

have to get some pages to Jerri—she always wants time to 'get into character.'"

Iola followed Sandy as she swept out of the cafeteria. "Catch you all in a bit," she said, waving to the Hardys and Chet.

They waved back and headed for the main soundstage. They arrived to find Rich Millani working furiously on one of the big control panels on the ship's bridge. Bruce Reid, Claudia Rajiv, and other cast members were standing around, studying their scripts, waiting for the problem to be corrected. Rod Webb was clutching a coffee cup so tightly that it was a wonder the cup didn't burst.

"How much longer?" Webb asked through clenched teeth. "The studio accountants are looking over our shoulders, you know."

"I'm working as fast as I can," Millani said.

"I'm here, Mr. Webb," Chet announced.

"Oh, good," said Ramon Torres, who was waiting with the rest of the actors. "Maybe you can help Rich fix the control panel."

"Cut the chatter, Torres," Webb said. "You'd be better off studying your part."

"But I don't have any lines," Torres replied.

"Lucky us," Webb said.

Torres crossed his arms over his chest and shot an angry look at Chet and the Hardys, as if they were at fault for his embarrassment.

73

It took another ten minutes for Rich Millani to correct the problem. Then shooting began at a furious pace.

As the morning wore on, tensions on the set grew. Actors flubbed more lines than they had the day before, and everyone acted nervous between takes. Chet, though, performed well.

"It's easy for me," he said during a break. "I don't have any lines."

"You do get to make a lot of threatening gestures, though," Iola observed. She had finished with makeup and was now a green-skinned alien from Betelgeuse.

The Mortons performed in several other scenes, including one where Iola and the other starship crew fled down a corridor away from the invading Slayer from Sirius.

Most of the principal actors were working this day. Jerri Bell and Geoff Gross appeared shortly after lunch and had to wait through a problem with the set lighting. Frank and Joe watched carefully but saw no sign of anyone causing trouble.

The light problem made the pace even more frantic. Between takes, Sandy O'Sullivan worked with Webb to try to tighten the storyline, to save shooting time and costs. They moved from the corridor set to the engine room for the next scene—a fight in which Lieutenant Commander Ravenscroft saved Ensign Allura from the Slayer.

"This is a great scene," Sandy whispered to the Hardys and Iola just before the final preparations were complete. "Chet's lucky he gets to play it."

"That's my brother," Iola said. "Just one big lucky guy."

Jerri Bell gave Chet a friendly smile. "Ready to go?" she asked.

"Mmm-hmm," Chet said, his reply muffled under the Slayer from Sirius helmet.

"Good luck," Jerri said, giving him a kiss on the side of the helmet and taking her place on the set.

The scenes with Bell and Gross went well, with both actors requiring few takes to hit their marks and get their lines down. Chet's lumbering entrance into the engine room went like a dream, too. He fired his Sirian blaster, and Bell's Ensign Allura fell to the floor, unconscious.

Gross, in his Lieutenant Commander Ravenscroft role, charged the Slayer. Chet swung around and, as planned in the script, swung the Slayer's armored fist toward Ravenscroft's face. But Chet and Gross miscalculated the blow.

Instead of coming up short, Chet's fist clipped the side of Gross's face. The Spacefleet officer fell to the engine room floor.

Before Webb could yell cut or Chet could apologize, Gross scrambled to his feet and smashed his shoulder into Chet's stomach.

8 Brawl in Warp Space

Chet staggered backward, more surprised than hurt. He dropped his blaster and landed heavily against one of the engine room consoles. As he hit the set, he pushed Gross away from him. The actor staggered but didn't go down. Instead, he came up swinging.

Instinctively, Chet brought up his hands and blocked the punch. Gross threw a couple of jabs at Chet's midsection, but the blows slid off the Slayer's fiberglass armor.

"Keep rolling!" Webb yelled. "This is great!"

"It's not in the script," Sandy said, a note of distress in her voice.

"Who cares, so long as they don't hurt each other," Webb replied. "It's perfect! Gross, Morton, keep going! We'll worry about removing the set noise in post-production."

Because Chet's face was hidden, the Hardys couldn't tell if he was concerned, but both brothers and Iola exchanged anxious glances. "Should we step in?" Joe whispered.

"I think Chet can handle himself," Frank replied.

"I hope he clobbers Gross!" Iola whispered.

If the Slayer's armor offered Chet some protection, it also slowed him down. Gross jabbed at him and then moved away as Chet swung clumsily at the muscular actor.

Gross aimed a kick at the Slayer's midsection. Chet caught the lieutenant commander's boot and heaved. Gross went sprawling, barely missing hitting his head on the warp core panel. He got back up with fire in his eyes.

"You may come from Sirius," Gross said, "but let's see how you like an old-fashioned Iowa knuckle sandwich!" The actor's punch clattered against the Slayer's helmet, and Chet staggered back.

"Great ad-lib!" Webb shouted. "We'll keep it."

"Rod," Sandy said, "I don't think our insurance company would like this."

"Just a little more," the director countered. "It's only improvisation."

Jerri Bell, lying on the floor of the engine room, whispered, "If one of them steps on me, I'm taking the rest of the day off!" She kept her eyes closed and hardly moved her lips when she spoke. Several stagehands, including Matt Stiller, chuckled. The coffee boy had paused in his gofer duties to watch the fight.

Chet blocked Gross's next punch and warded off a kick with the Slayer's right shin guard. Chet countered with a powerful shove. Gross staggered back into a panel, which shorted out in a display of sparks.

"Great!" Webb yelled.

Snarling, Gross ran forward, but this time Chet was ready for him. When Gross came in, Chet ducked and grabbed the front of the lieutenant commander's uniform. With a mighty heave, he lifted Gross off the floor like a pro wrestler about to body slam an opponent.

"Marvelous!" Webb cried.

Chet tried to throw Gross, but the actor grabbed the collar of the Slayer's armor. As Chet lurched under the actor's weight, Gross slammed his knee into the Slayer's helmet.

The assembled cast and crew gasped. Chet staggered to his knees. Gross twisted out of his grasp and kicked Chet in his armored chest. The Slayer fell over backward with a resounding thud. Gross moved in, ready to kick him again.

"That's enough," Joe said. Before Gross could follow through, Joe and Frank stepped in front of the cameras and between the enraged actor and their friend. Gross glared at them.

"Cut!" Webb yelled. "Cut! Who said those two could step in? They wrecked my shot."

"Um, Rod . . ." Sandy said, holding up her script and pointing to a section of it.

Webb slapped his forehead. "Right! Right!" he said. "Geoff, didn't you read the script? You don't defeat the Slayer in this scene."

"Sorry," Gross said. "I guess I got carried away." He stepped back and wiped the sweat from his forehead.

"Don't worry about it," Webb said, beaming. "We'll figure out a different ending, right, Sandy?"

"Um, sure," Sandy said.

Webb was still smiling. "This," he said, "is why I always keep three cameras rolling."

Chet lay on his back, wriggling like an over-turned tortoise. He pulled off his helmet. "Help me!" he said. "This suit isn't made for getting up."

Joe and Frank gave him a hand. "You okay, Chet?" Frank whispered.

"I'm fine," Chet said. "I just couldn't move in the costume is all."

As Chet rose, the impromptu audience of cast and crew applauded. "Good work, Morton," Bruce Reid said.

Jerri Bell got up from the engine room floor and dusted herself off. "Peck Wilson could hardly have done better," she said. "Though next time I hope you boys will tell me when you're going to improvise. That way, I can fall in a more comfortable position." She rubbed her hip where she had landed on it.

"Are you kidding?" Geoff Gross said. "This guy is an accident waiting to happen. He could have hurt me with some of those stunts."

"That goes double for you," Chet said. "You were the one who started it. And I think you may have cracked the helmet."

"Better the helmet than your head," Iola said quietly.

"Calm down, boys," Claudia Rajiv said. "It all worked out fine. Nobody got hurt, and Rod got some great shots."

Director Webb nodded. "True," he said. Then turning to the Hardys he added, "But next time you step in before I yell 'Cut,' I'll have you run off the lot."

Joe stepped forward as if to say something, but Frank held him back.

"I don't think that will be necessary, Rod," Sandy said. "Why doesn't everyone take fifteen to calm down a bit."

"Yeah, okay," Webb said. "Let's take our dinner break. I want everyone to be fresh when we start again. This may be another long night. And, Morton, have Stan Pekar look at that helmet. We don't want it splitting in half during a crucial scene."

Chet nodded his agreement and headed for the makeup room. Gross and most of the other cast members drifted off to their dressing rooms. Before he left, Webb pulled Matt Stiller aside. "Find Millani and have him fix the damage to the set. I still want to get a few shots in if we can."

"Right," Stiller said, and ran off.

"Well, that was certainly exciting," Iola said.

"More exciting than I would prefer," Sandy O'Sullivan said. "Now I have to do more rewrites!"

"Don't worry, Sandy," Claudia Rajiv said. "I'm sure you can handle it."

"Claudia," Sandy replied, "I'm not sure if I can handle *anything* extra right now."

"If you have to go, we can look after ourselves," Iola said.

"Actually, I can look after them," Claudia said.

"Great," Sandy said. "I'll be right here figuring out how to fit that fight into the rest of the story."

"Come on, folks," Claudia said. "Let's give the girl some space. Let's go eat."

"Sounds good," said Frank.

"Everyone knows we're really behind on shooting this episode," Claudia said confidentially. "Some of the studio accountants have been prowling around, threatening to shut the show down if things don't shape up."

"Could they do that?" Joe asked.

Claudia shrugged. "Everyone working on the show thinks that *Warp Space* could be the next big hit. We've got a good cast and crew, and the start of a solid fan base. But we don't have the ratings—not yet. If the show runs over budget too much more, we may never get the chance to build that audience."

Hearing the conversation, Bruce Reid walked over to the group. "The accountants see everything in terms of dollars and cents," Reid said. "They don't care if the show makes money next year; they want it to make money now. If they think we're bleeding cash, they'll pull the plug."

"Fan support is critical," Claudia said, "but it can't stop the money men if they think we're a lost cause."

"Speaking of fans," Bruce said, "I need to catch up on my e-mail. I'll see you all after dinner."

"See you, Bruce," Claudia said. She and the Hardys and Iola headed for the cafeteria.

As they stood in line to get their food, Iola asked, "What was up with Geoff Gross there? He might have hurt Chet."

"Geoff's always been a macho hothead," Claudia replied. "He's convinced that he should be the star of the show. Plus, he's pretty sweet on Jerri. He's probably a bit jealous of the time Chet's been spending with her."

"Boy, the one time Chet does okay with a girl, it *still* messes up his life," Joe said.

"Everyone seems on edge," Frank said. "Except maybe you."

Claudia shrugged. "I've been out of work before," she said, "and I'll be out of work again. Don't get me wrong, I want this show to succeed, but my life doesn't begin and end with it." They sat down to eat.

"Do you think someone could be trying to hurt the show on purpose?" Joe asked.

"Like who?" Claudia replied.

"We're not sure," Frank said, "but a lot of things have been going wrong lately."

"I think it's just the pressure," Claudia said. "That's why I'm throwing a party tomorrow night, so everyone can let off some steam. You guys are welcome to come if you like."

"We'd love to," Iola said, sipping her drink through a straw so as not to smudge her makeup.

They finished their food and headed back toward the soundstage. The frantic shooting had eaten up much of the day. Already long, twilight shadows darkened the lot.

As they passed by Bruce Reid's trailer, he came out, looking distraught. "Have you seen the Web site today?" he asked Claudia. "Do you know anything about this?"

"Know anything about what?" she asked.

"Come in," Reid said. "I'll show you." He ushered Claudia, the Hardys, and Iola into his trailer.

The group huddled around a laptop on the trailer's counter.

"I was checking my mail on my fan site," Reid explained, "and discovered a lot of sympathy notes. Some angry ones, too. At first I couldn't figure out what it was all about. Finally, I tracked it back to the main *Warp Space* site." His fingers flew over the keyboard, pulling up a new Web site. "Take a look!" he said forlornly.

"I don't see anything different," Claudia said, checking the brightly colored front page of the *Warp Space* Web site.

"It's in the news items, near the bottom of the page—the bottom!" Reid said.

The Hardys and Iola leaned closer as Claudia scrolled down.

Near the bottom of the page, was a picture of Reid. Next to the picture, was a simple block of black and white text.

"Captain Winter no more—Bruce Reid leaving series."

9 Webs of Intrigue

"You're leaving the series?" Iola asked.

"Not that I know of," Reid said, wiping the sweat from his forehead with a handkerchief.

Frank reached over and clicked the link on the headline. "It says here that you've decided to move on because of creative differences," he said.

Reid rolled his eyes and moaned. "That's a death knell for an actor!" he said. "'Creative differences' always means an actor is difficult to work with. But I *haven't* been difficult. I've given my all for this show."

Claudia put her hand comfortingly on his shoulder. "Everyone knows that, Bruce," she said.

"It also says that the fate of your character remains up in the air," Joe added.

"It does," Reid said, "but I read on a fan site that Captain Winter will be killed two episodes after the one we're shooting now. Then Ensign Allura gets a field promotion and becomes captain for a while."

"How can that be true?" Claudia asked. "I don't think Sandy has two episodes done beyond this one. We both know she's still sweating over re-writes on *this* episode."

"But we also know she has a master plan for the series in her head," Reid said. "If she *is* bumping my character off, she might have leaked the news to soften the blow—or put it up herself using a pseudonym."

"Mr. Reid, I think you're worrying for nothing," Iola said. "How could they kill Captain Winter? He's the emotional center of the show."

"You know how this happened," Reid said, ignoring Iola and pacing the trailer. "A lot of Web sites upload their news weeks in advance, and then the program displays it on the proper date. Sandy must have decided to write me out but hadn't gotten around to telling me about it yet. The show's ratings have been marginal. A stunt like this might perk them up."

"Or it could be just a prank," Joe said. He shot Frank a look that said, if it were a prank, he didn't think it was very funny.

"O'Sullivan and Webb authorize everything that goes up on the site," Reid said. "Sandy writes most of it herself. Why would the creator and head writer put it up on the site if it weren't true?"

"Sandy doesn't post everything herself," Claudia said.

Reid sat down and put his head in his hands. "I need this job," he said. "My last series tanked, and I really need *Warp Space* to fly. I'm not getting any younger, you know. And the rest of the actors around here are sharks—except for you, Claudia."

"There's an easy way to settle this," Frank said. "Go to Sandy and ask her."

"But what if it's true?"

"Better to find out now than spend time anguishing over it," Joe said.

Reid stood up and took a deep breath. "Yeah. You're right."

"That's the old Captain Winter spirit!" Iola said, clapping him on the shoulder. He smiled at her.

"We'd better get back to the set," Claudia said. "Webb's probably having kittens by now. I'm in the next shot, too."

"But I'm not," Reid said. "I'll find Sandy and talk to her."

"We'll be happy to go with you," Joe said, "and lend some moral support."

Reid nodded. "Thanks, kids. I appreciate it. The

show's pretty lucky that your friend won the contest."

They all left Reid's trailer and went back through the lengthening shadows to the soundstage. As it turned out, shooting hadn't started again. Rich Millani was still repairing damage from the earlier fight. Webb had even called Stan Pekar in to help Millani after Pekar finished working on Chet's helmet.

Sandy wasn't there, though, so Reid and the Hardys went to look for her. Iola stayed behind because she had a walk-through in the next set of shots.

"Sandy's probably in her office," Reid said, leading the brothers across the studio to the brick building that housed the production offices.

"Mr. Reid," Joe said, "do you think someone could be trying to sabotage the series?"

"I don't know," Reid said. "There's been a lot of strange stuff going on around here lately, that's for sure."

"What kind of strange stuff?" Frank asked.

"Like the accident that put Wilson in the hospital," Reid said. "There have been a lot of repairs, too—things are wearing out or being damaged faster than normal. Props have gone missing as well. All of this is contributing to the show's budget crunch, and that's made everyone—including me—jumpy. Whether any of it is deliberate, though . . ." He shrugged.

Though darkness now covered the eerily silent

lot, a light still burned in the old brick building that housed Sandy's office.

"Looks like she's in," Joe said.

They walked through an empty reception room and knocked on a door that said Sandy O'Sullivan—Executive Producer.

"Come in," Sandy's voice called.

They entered an office piled high with papers, scripts, books, and memorabilia. Most of the souvenirs were from *Warp Space*, but there was a smattering from other SF shows as well. In the middle of the mess, Sandy O'Sullivan sat slumped over a laptop computer, typing furiously. She looked up as they entered.

"Are we back shooting?" she asked, panic flashing across her gray eyes for a moment. "I'm still adjusting the plot to incorporate the new fight footage." She kept typing.

"Not yet. In a few minutes," Frank said.

"Before then, though," Reid said, "we need to talk."

Sandy stopped typing. "Talk? About what? Could we possibly do this later? I'm insanely busy at the moment."

"Sandy, are you firing me?" Reid asked. "Are you killing off my character?"

"What?" Sandy asked, surprised.

"The official Web site says that I'm leaving the show," Reid said.

"And some fan sites are reporting that Captain Winter will be killed off and replaced by Ensign Allura," Joe added.

Sandy burst out laughing. "That's the most absurd thing I've ever heard!" she said. "Bruce, without you there is no *Warp Space*."

"Why is the information on the official site, then?" Frank asked. "Mr. Reid said that everything on the site is cleared through the producer's office."

"That's true," Sandy said. "The Webmasters live in Renton, Washington, but everything that goes up has to be cleared from here. That's how I know that nothing of the kind is on the site." Her fingers flew over her keyboard and she quickly connected to the *Warp Space* site. When the Web page came up, she scowled. "We've been hacked!" she said.

"Well, that's a relief," Reid said. "I was worried that you might bump off Captain Winter as a publicity stunt."

"Bruce," Sandy said, "you should know me better than that. I feel about Captain Winter the way I feel about my dad."

"Who has the password for uploading to the site?" Joe asked.

"The Webmasters, of course, and Rod and I have it as well," Sandy said. "So do the studio offices. I've got it written down somewhere . . . um"—she reached for a sticky note on the corner of her desk blotter— "here." She grinned sheepishly.

"Not a very secure system," Frank said. "Anyone could have seen it there."

"I suppose," Sandy said. "Until now it didn't occur to me that anyone would *want* to hack the site. A lot of people go through this office on any given day. I shouldn't have left the password out. What a dope I am!"

"Beefing up security all around would probably be a good idea," Joe said.

Sandy nodded. "Yeah. Given the troubles we've been having, I guess it would. Rats! Who needs this extra pressure?"

"Not me, that's for sure," Reid said.

"Do me a favor," Sandy said. "Don't mention this to anyone. The last thing we need is the studio bosses getting wind of more troubles on the show. I've had a hard time keeping them—and the media—out of our hair as it is. One more fiasco and the studio may decide to shut us down."

"Don't worry," Frank replied. "Joe and I have kept a few secrets in our day."

"Good," Sandy said. "I'll have the Web guys fix that page before it can go any further."

"Too bad we can't rein in the fan sites the same way," Reid said.

"We'll send out an official release denying the rumor, and— Oh, no!" Sandy said. "The shoot! We need to get back!" She ran across the office and pulled some new script pages out of her printer.

Then she sprinted out the door. "I'll take care of the Web site on the next break," she called back.

"Full ahead, warp speed," Joe said jokingly. He, Frank, and Reid followed Sandy out.

When they returned to the set, they found Chet and Gross working on retakes for the fight. This time, though, both the Slayer and the lieutenant commander fought with more caution and less enthusiasm. Everyone on the set looked tired, but nothing indicated that the shooting would end anytime soon.

"Looks like it's going to be another long night," Reid said.

Webb shot them a stern look as they entered, then perked up when he saw Sandy. As they wrapped the take, Sandy went over to consult with the director.

Iola sidled over to Chet. "How's it going?" she asked.

"Pretty slowly," he replied, his voice muffled by the slayer's helmet.

"In that case," Joe said, "I think Frank and I will poke around a little bit, see if we can turn up anything on the troubles the show's been having."

"Be careful," Iola said.

"Take good care of Chet," Frank replied with a grin.

"I heard that," Chet said.

As the actors got organized for the next take,

Frank and Joe quietly left the starship's engine room. They wandered through the soundstage, checking out the other sets.

"The main question I see here," Frank said, as they walked past the shuttle bay, "is who has something to gain from the show's problems."

"You'd think that no one would have anything to gain," Joe said. "If the show gets shut down, everyone loses."

"Maybe this stuff isn't intended to get the show shut down, though," Frank said. "Maybe it's all some kind of crazy publicity stunt."

"Could be," Joe said. "I know that some people think that *any* publicity is good publicity. It might even be to Reid's advantage to stir up some rumors about himself. The attention could help his sagging career."

Frank nodded. "Yeah. You could make the same kind of argument for Jerri Bell, Geoff Gross, Ramon Torres, or even Claudia Rajiv. Plus, any of the characters might be promoted to captain if Reid left. The show itself could benefit from extra publicity, too."

"Sandy seems to be trying to keep all the trouble quiet, though," Joe said. "If the show is really on the edge, this kind of publicity could backfire and shut everything down."

"Which brings us back to who would benefit if that happens," Frank said. They meandered through the darkened ship's infirmary, toward the bridge set.

"I still think Gross and Torres are strong candidates," Joe said. "They're both hotheaded, and we've seen that tendency override their team spirit already."

"Hold it!" Frank said quietly, coming to a sudden stop.

"What?" Joe whispered.

Frank said nothing but pointed to the bridge set, only a few yards away. The set was nearly as dark as the infirmary. A handful of lights from the ship's control panels cast a dim, multicolored glow around the room.

As the brothers watched, a shadowy shape rose up from behind one panel and slipped over to the next. As it crossed through the pale lights, the Hardys got a good look at the intruder. The prowler stalking the bridge was *not* human.

10 Beneath the Mask

The creature moving between the control panels had pointed ears, two stubby antennae, and scaly blue skin. The thing didn't spot the brothers as they watched it. It quietly moved to the next console and stuck its inhuman head under the panel.

"Looks like we may have our saboteur," Joe whispered. He grinned slyly. "It figures that it'd be someone from outer space."

"We don't have him yet," Frank replied quietly. "But if you slip behind the next set over we can come at him from two sides. There's no way he can escape, whoever he might be under that makeup."

Joe nodded his agreement with the plan and silently moved around to the other side of the set. When he reached the opposite end of the bridge, he signaled to Frank and both of them stepped out from their concealment.

"Hold it right there!" Frank said.

"This is the last set you'll sabotage!" Joe added.

The alien jumped at the sound of their voices but held the screwdriver tightly in his scaly blue hand.

"Drop the screwdriver," Joe said. "Don't make this tougher on yourself than it has to be.

"W-What?" the alien sputtered.

Frank took a step closer and assumed a martial arts attack stance. "We mean it," he said. "Drop the screwdriver!"

The alien did as he was told. "Okay, okay. No need to get violent. It's just me," he said, pulling his mask off, "Stan Pekar."

"What are you doing messing with the set?" Frank asked.

The wiry special-effects man took a deep breath and sat down in the command chair. "Boy," he said, "you guys really gave me a scare. Warn a fellow next time, okay? I wasn't 'messing' with the set, I was *fixing* it. With all the troubles we've had lately, Rich Millani is running behind on repairs, so he asked me to pitch in."

"In the dark?" Frank said.

"You can't fix the faults in these luminous panels with the overhead lights on," Pekar said. "The big lamps blind you, making it hard to locate the problem. That's why I was using a flashlight." He pointed to where the flashlight lay on the floor.

"How do we know you're telling the truth?" Joe asked.

Pekar frowned. "Ask Rich, if you want," he said. "Unless maybe you're of the same opinion that Rod Webb is—that Rich and I are working together to rip off the show."

"Are you?" asked Frank.

"Of course not," Pekar scoffed. "Why would I jeopardize my reputation for a penny-ante operation like this? I don't need this job. I came out of semiretirement because the show sounded like fun. It hasn't been a lot of laughs lately, though. Why are you guys so interested in this? You're on the set for only a week, and you don't even have a walk-on."

"We're concerned for the cast and crew," Joe said. "If this show folds, it'll take a lot of good folks down with it, not to mention the fans who'd be disappointed."

"And that's not even counting Chet and Iola," Frank added. "So long as they're involved, we can't just walk away."

"Yeah," Pekar said. "I know how you feel. That kind of loyalty's kept me going, too. Now, though, I'm beginning to wonder if it's all worth it."

"You've been involved with movies and TV for a long time," Frank said. "What's your take on all this?"

"Well," Pekar said, "I've been around since most

of the people working on *Warp Space* were in diapers. I remember when Rod Webb was lurking around sets doing pickup gaffer and grip work. My career was in full swing when Bruce Reid was a teen heartthrob on *Hunk High School* and Claudia Rajiv was doing lollipop commercials. So, yeah, I've seen a lot."

"And . . ." Joe prodded. He took a seat behind one of the consoles near the command chair. Frank did the same.

Pekar shrugged again. "*Warp Space* is no better or worse than most TV shows in terms of personnel. There's a lot of talent here, sure, but there are a lot of social climbers as well. Most of the folks involved with the show will do anything to get ahead."

"Not you, though," Frank said.

"When you've got a couple of Oscars on your shelf, you don't have to look for work," Pekar said. "Most of this is just old hat to me, but I still find it fun. When I don't, I'll retire again."

"Do you think that'll be soon?" Joe asked.

"It depends on the day," Pekar said. "Most days, I'm having a blast. Other days it's just one crisis after another. Some days, like today, I start out doing makeup and end up jury-rigging together electronic gizmos."

"You and Millani work on the electronics together, right?" Frank said.

Pekar nodded. "Yeah. Doing production work on props and stuff is a lot of fun. The annoying part is how many things disappear around here. Some, like the insignia that fell off the Slayer's outfit during the fire the other day, are just normal production accidents." He shrugged again. "Nothing you can do about that kind of stuff. Other things, though . . . Well, let's just say that I'm pretty sure someone around here has light fingers."

"And Rod Webb thinks it's you and Millani?" Joe asked.

"Not exactly," Pekar said, scowling. "He thinks we're cutting production on the props and skimming the cost savings for ourselves. Underproducing and skimming would be a stupid idea for someone in my profession. My clients have to trust me to work reliably within a budget. But Rod's had stupid ideas before, and I'm sure this won't be his last one."

"It sounds like you don't care for him much," Frank said.

"He's okay—for a director," Pekar said. "Most of the cast and crew are wrapped up in their own problems; Rod's no different. If the show sinks, his wallet takes a hit; if it flies, he's locked into a long contract, which limits his options. It's the same with the rest of the cast. Even when they win, they lose. Right now, the show is in limbo. The crew can't count on the income continuing, but they can't start looking for other work, either. That's why everybody's so edgy. If things don't calm down soon, though, it could become a self-fulfilling prophecy. *Warp Space* could disintegrate on its own even before the studio accountants pull the plug."

Pekar stood up and stretched. "Personally, I'm not too concerned. I'll either land on my feet or go gracefully into retirement—again. I'd be a happier man, though, if I could figure out where those missing props and souvenirs are going. Nearly everyone has lost something."

"We'll keep an eye out for the missing stuff," Joe said.

Pekar chuckled. "Good luck. You guys seem to know what you're doing, but showbiz is a world of its own. Almost no one plays it straight in this business. Everyone has hidden motives and agendas."

"Everyone but you?" Frank said.

"Yeah," Pekar said, smiling. "Everybody but me."

"We found a smashed Slayer from Sirius figurine the other day," Joe said. "Was that one of the missing items?"

"It could be," Pekar said. "I think more of those figurines went missing from the studio offices than actually got used for promotion. One day they'll turn up at an online auction site, I'm sure. Or maybe we've just got a giant mutant packrat running around the lot."

"Speaking of giant mutants," Frank said, "what's with the disguise?"

"Oh, this?" Pekar said, holding up the blue, scaly mask. "It's something new I'm trying out. Makeup is a long and expensive process. Masks, on the other hand, are quick and easy. We could save both time and money if we used more alien masks on the show. The trouble is, masks usually look phony on camera."

"That one looked pretty realistic," Joe said. "We could almost believe you were a real alien skulking around the set."

Pekar smiled. "Yeah, good. That's the effect I wanted. It's easy to move around in and see out of, too. That's why I was wearing it to do repairs—kind of a torture test. We'll see how it holds up under the lights, though."

Frank and Joe stood. "Well, good luck with that," Joe said.

"Yeah, thanks," Pekar replied. "Hey, I need to get back to work on these panels. If I don't, Rich will have to do it before shooting starts tomorrow."

"No problem," Frank said. "Thanks for talking to us."

"My pleasure," Pekar said. "Next time, though, give me some warning before you sneak up on me. A heart attack would end my career quicker than a hundred angry directors."

The brothers laughed and headed for the shooting set; Pekar went back to his work.

The Hardys arrived at the engine room just as shooting wrapped for the night. All the actors looked exhausted, and director Webb seemed worn out, too.

"See you all bright and early tomorrow," Sandy said, trying to appear more energetic than she looked. "We made good progress today," she added.

"But we're still behind schedule, and dangerously close to breaking the budget with overtime costs," Webb put in. "Remember, we've got shooting at the park again at the end of the week, too. So, everyone be on top of your game tomorrow. Go home. Get some rest." With this last comment, he looked pointedly at Claudia and Jerri. "I know that's what *I* intend to do," he finished.

"Me, too," Sandy said. "I could sleep for a week. But until four or five A.M. will have to do."

"See you all in the morning," Bruce Reid said. The others muttered their goodbyes; most headed for home, though some—Chet and Iola included—went to the makeup room. There, Marge Nelson quickly removed their prosthetics and paints.

Less than an hour later, the Hardys and the Mortons returned to the trailer they were sharing. Iola and Chet quickly collapsed onto their beds.

"Acting is hard work!" Iola said.

"You expected all bright lights and glamour?" Joe asked.

"Well, we're getting those, too," she said. "Or at least my brother is."

Chet put his hands behind his head and smiled. "Well, I *did* enter you in the contest, after all. It's only fair that I share in the prize."

"You got your share of lumps, too," Frank said.

"Yeah," Chet said. "What is up with Geoff Gross? Is he just a creep, or what?"

"There's no way to tell, yet," Joe said. "We'll keep poking around, though. Someone's behind all these troubles in *Warp Space*. It's only a matter of time before we figure out who."

Chet rolled over. "Would you grab me a soda out of the fridge, Frank?" he asked. "I'm too pooped to walk across the room. I think even my bruises have bruises."

"Sure thing," Frank said. He walked to the trailer's small fridge and opened the door, then frowned. "We're out. They must not have restocked it today."

"Ah, the disadvantages of being extras!" Iola said. "I bet Jerri Bell has fresh soda in her trailer every day."

"It's no problem," Joe said. "I'll walk to the vending machines by the cafeteria and get some."

"Hurry back," Chet said.

Joe left the trailer and headed for the closed cafeteria. Before he'd gone too far, though, a light from the production office caught his eye. The light played across the window like a flashlight beam. Someone was inside the office looking for something.

Before Joe could investigate further, though, the light snapped off and the door to the office opened. A lithe figure stepped out into the shadows. Hoping for a better look, Joe followed. The intruder stuck to the shadows, moving quickly but keeping out of sight.

Joe trailed the shadowy figure all the way back to the soundstage. The figure sneaked inside; Joe did the same.

Moving cautiously, Joe followed the soft sounds of footsteps toward the bridge stage. There, he saw a familiar alien figure inspecting one of the ship's control panels.

Breathing a sigh of relief, Joe walked forward.

"Hey, Mr. Pekar," he said. "Are you still working? I thought everyone had gone home."

The man in the blue-scaled alien mask spun around and punched Joe square in the face.

11 Battle on the Bridge

Joe staggered back, more shocked than hurt.

Before the younger Hardy could recover, the alien dropped into a crouch and sweep-kicked Joe behind the knees. Joe landed hard on the floor of the bridge. The set's thin carpeting did little to cushion the blow.

Joe tried to get to his feet, but the alien pushed a console over on top of him. The painted plywood and plastic hit Joe hard, leaving a long scrape down his left arm. The alien turned to flee.

"Oh, no you don't!" Joe said. From under the console he grabbed the toe of the alien's sneaker.

The alien tripped and sprawled headlong into the command seat. The seat rocked precariously but didn't fall over. Joe pushed the toppled console aside and scrambled to his feet.

Joe threw a punch at the alien, but the blue-masked man spun the command chair around. Joe's knuckles cracked against the chair's high back as the alien jumped to his feet and hopped over the control panel behind the chair.

Rather than hurdle the panel, Joe raced to the left, heading for a gap between the command stations. The alien saw him coming, picked up a nearby chair, and flung it at Joe.

Joe ducked and the chair struck the command station to his left. The panel exploded in a shower of sparks, momentarily blinding Joe. While he recovered, the alien dashed for the door at the back of the bridge. But the door mechanism jammed, and he couldn't get through.

Brushing the sparks out of his hair, Joe ran for the door as well. As the alien turned to face him, Joe hit his quarry with a flying tackle.

The two of them smashed through the thin plywood door and into the fake elevator beyond. The alien tried to knee Joe in the chin, but Joe rolled away. Both combatants scrambled to their feet.

The masked man pulled a circuit panel off the elevator wall and hurled it at Joe. Joe batted the plastic box aside and came at the alien again.

The younger Hardy threw a punch at the alien's blue face. But the masked man ducked, grabbed

Joe's arm, and turned Joe's momentum against him.

Before Joe could recover, the alien used a judo move to smash him into the elevator wall. The wall gave way, and Joe fell onto the hard concrete beyond. He landed awkwardly on his shoulder, wincing with the impact. Gritting his teeth, he got to his feet, but by that time the intruder had run back into the bridge set. Joe exited the elevator just in time to see the intruder run off the set and into the darkness.

Joe sprinted after him, trying to keep track of his foe in the dim light. The alien led Joe back toward the shuttle bay set. The intruder moved quickly in the darkness, easily dodging around the equipment littering the stage.

The alien ducked into the shuttle bay, with Joe close on his heels. Joe darted through a set door to go after his foe, but tripped over a long cable stretched across the doorway. As he fell forward, he heard the creak of a portable light stand giving way. He looked up to see the light falling straight toward his head.

A figure stepped from the shadows and grabbed the stand, stopping its fall.

"Frank!" Joe said. "Am I glad to see you!"

Frank smiled. "I got worried when you didn't come back right away," the elder Hardy said. "I went looking and the stage door was open. I heard a commotion and came inside."

"It's Pekar," Joe said, scrambling to his feet. "He

jumped me and we fought. I chased him in here."

"He led you into a trap," Frank concluded. "I saw him run out as I came in. Come on. We can still catch him."

Both brothers ran for the exit on the far side of the set. "Cable!" Joe yelled as they reached the entrance to the engine room set. Frank glanced down in time to see the trap before he tripped over it. He jumped over the cable and through the set's door.

As he landed, something heavy crashed down on his head. Stars burst before his eyes, and he staggered forward, barely able to stand.

Joe charged through the door just as the alien raised the fire extinguisher to hit Frank again. The younger Hardy hammered his fist into the intruder's gut. The alien dropped the heavy metal cylinder and lurched backward.

Joe dodged the extinguisher as it fell, and lunged at the alien. But the intruder spun, aiming a sweeping kick at Joe's head. Joe ducked and threw a punch toward the alien's blue face. The younger Hardy's fist connected with the intruder's chin.

The alien fell back but brought his knee up into Joe's midsection. The air rushed out of Joe's lungs, and he fell to the floor. The alien turned and climbed up a service ladder leading to the balcony level of the set.

"You didn't tell me he knew kung fu," Frank said as both brothers staggered to their feet.

"It must have slipped my mind when he kicked me in the head," Joe replied. "You go left, I'll go right. We'll trap him on the upper level." The brothers split up, Joe climbing the same ladder that the alien had used. Frank headed for the ladder on the opposite side of the room.

As the brothers climbed, the alien sprinted around the engine room's circular balcony. He reached some rigging cables dangling halfway between the ladders and began to climb up toward an overhead catwalk.

Joe was faster than his foe had reckoned. The younger Hardy reached the upper level in seconds and spotted a toolbox lying by one of the panels on the floor. Snatching it up, he heaved it at the intruder.

The alien saw the box coming and let go of the cables just in time. As the alien dropped to the balcony floor, the toolbox flew over his head and crashed behind him against the set wall.

As Joe charged forward, the alien grabbed the rigging cables and snapped them like a whip. The cables lashed forward and wrapped themselves around Joe's neck and chest. Joe grabbed at the cables to keep them from choking him. The alien kicked at him, and Joe staggered back out of the way. The tangled cables made it difficult for the younger Hardy to maneuver.

Fortunately, Frank arrived at that moment and charged at the intruder. The elder Hardy ducked under the alien's spin kick and responded with a karate chop to the masked man's knee. The intruder grunted, but kept his feet.

Joe tugged on the cables, trying to free himself, but his action had the opposite effect. A panel in the ceiling pulled off, nearly hitting Joe in the head, and a huge mass of tangled wires fell down around the younger Hardy. Several of the wires sparked and smoked as they broke loose. It was all Joe could do to avoid them, and to stay out of Frank's way.

The alien spun and tried to kick Frank in the head. Frank ducked back and responded with a sweep kick of his own. He caught the alien at the ankle and the masked man fell onto his back.

"Frank, help!" Joe gasped. Struggling with the sparking wires, he'd become even more enmeshed in the cables. Now the younger Hardy tottered per-ilously close to the balcony railing.

Frank grabbed Joe's shirt to keep him from falling backward. Those few seconds were all the alien needed to regain his feet. As Frank steadied his brother, the alien kicked the elder Hardy hard in the back.

Frank toppled forward over the balcony railing.

"Frank!" Joe called. He reached out, but the

tangled cables kept him from catching his falling brother.

Fortunately, Frank's grasping fingers caught the edge of the balcony floor as he fell past. His fingertips dug into the carpeting, but his grip wasn't solid.

Frank knew that the twenty-foot drop to the studio floor probably wouldn't kill him. On the other hand, he would be lucky to escape without any broken bones. He tried to squeeze the carpet harder, but the nap of the fabric kept slipping from his grasp.

"Hang on, Frank!" Joe called.

Working frantically, Joe yanked himself free from the cables just as Frank lost his grip on the edge.

Joe lunged forward and grabbed for Frank's hands as they started slipping away. The younger Hardy caught hold of his brother's fingers and squeezed tight. Frank's fingers began to pull free.

The older Hardy winced in pain as Joe tightened his grip. Then, with a mighty heave, Joe slowly pulled his brother up to the balcony.

Frank scrambled over the railing, immediately looking for the intruder. "Pekar's gone," he said, exasperation tingeing his voice.

"Well, it was either let him get away or let you drop," Joe said.

Frank smiled slightly. "Glad you made the right choice."

They climbed down from the engine room balcony and looked around but saw no trace of the intruder. Before they left the set, though, Chet and Iola came in.

"What are you guys up to?" Iola asked. "You were gone so long we got worried and decided to look for you."

"Oh, just fighting for our lives against Stan Pekar," Joe said.

"The makeup man?" Chet asked.

"Yeah," Frank said. "It looks like he may have been behind the sabotage after all."

"He pulled a stunt on me that was pretty similar to when you tripped over that light stand in the park, Iola," Joe said.

"But it doesn't make any sense," she said. "Stan Pekar has a long and distinguished career in TV and film."

Chet shrugged. "Hey, sometimes folks just go crazy," he said. "Or maybe he's having money troubles or other problems we don't know about."

"I'll admit, he wasn't at the top of my suspects list," Frank said, "but I've got the bruises to prove he was up to no good."

"So, where is he?" Chet asked.

"He got away," Joe said, "after pushing Frank off the engine room balcony."

"Good thing Joe caught me," Frank said, "though I wish we could have stopped Pekar, too."

"Maybe he's still on the lot," Iola suggested. "We should call the front gate."

"Good idea," said Joe. They found a studio phone and called the guard post. "We're in luck," he said, hanging up. "They say Pekar hasn't left."

"Let's find him, then," Chet said. "We'll split up and—"

"No," Frank said. "He's a kung fu expert. We should stick together."

"Maybe he headed for the makeup room," Iola said.

"That would make sense," Joe said. "He'd probably want to remove his mask, as well as cover up any other evidence before leaving."

The teens walked through the darkened soundstage toward the door leading to the makeup room in the adjoining brick building.

They hadn't gone too far, though, when Iola spotted someone hunkered in the shadows beside the stage wall. Joe and Frank sprinted forward, ready to resume their fight.

"All right, Pekar," Joe said, "this is where you get your comeuppance!"

Pekar was sitting on the floor, leaning against the wall with his legs splayed out in front of him. He didn't respond.

"Joe," Frank said, "he's out cold."

12 A Shocking Turn

"How can he be unconscious?" Chet said. "You said he was fighting with you just a few minutes ago."

"Maybe we hurt him more than we thought," Joe suggested.

"I don't think so, Joe," Frank said. "If he passed out after the fight, where's his mask?"

"What mask?" Iola asked.

"The alien getup we saw him in earlier," Joe said. "He was wearing it when we fought."

"Well, I don't see it anywhere," Chet said.

"He was wearing gloves when we fought, too," Frank said.

Joe nodded. "But he's not now. And his clothes are different."

"He's coming around," Iola said.

Sure enough, Stan Pekar coughed and his eyes fluttered open. "Who hit me?" he asked groggily.

Frank and Joe looked at each other. "You mean in the engine room?" Frank asked.

"Engine room?" Pekar said groggily. "What are you talking about?"

Frank's eyes narrowed. "Didn't you just . . . *see* us on the engine room set?"

Pekar shook his head and winced. "I don't think so. I'd finished with the sets and was headed back to makeup. . . . Then suddenly I'm seeing stars." He gingerly rubbed the back of his skull.

"Did you leave your mask somewhere?" Joe asked.

"No, I'm still . . ." Pekar touched his face with his fingers. "Hey! Where's my mask?"

"Someone took it," Frank said.

"And then got into a running battle with us throughout the soundstage," Joe added.

"Did you get him?" Pekar asked. He struggled to stand. Chet and Iola helped him to his feet.

"No," Frank said. "He got away."

"Not before busting up some sets, though," Joe added.

Pekar rolled his eyes. "Oh, no! That's the last thing we need!"

"We thought we were fighting you," Frank said. "He was wearing your mask."

"I wouldn't last two rounds with you guys," Pekar said.

"Well, this guy went the distance," Joe said, "and then some. We were lucky to get away with just bruises."

"Big guy, was he?" Pekar asked. He was looking more alert by the moment.

"Not really," Frank said, and realized the man they had been fighting was much slimmer than Pekar. "But he knew what he was doing in a fight."

"He knew his way around the sets, too," Joe said.

Pekar rubbed the back of his head again. "I'd say he was pretty good at clubbing people from behind, as well."

"Why'd he take the mask, though?" Frank asked.

"Maybe he didn't want to be recognized," Iola suggested. "Though who'd be around to recognize him this late, I don't know."

"The studio's not going to like this," Pekar said. He called security, and security called Webb and O'Sullivan, both of whom quickly arrived on the set.

"We'd better not tell the studio execs tonight," Webb said.

A very sleepy Sandy O'Sullivan nodded. "No need to wake them with bad news about the show. We can alert them in the morning."

"We really should call the police," Joe said.

Sandy shook her head. "If the police get involved, it'll slow production further," she said.

"And attract the attention of the news media," Webb added, suppressing a yawn. "We don't need reporters poking around. We've got enough trouble meeting our schedule as it is. If we're not careful, this could be the end of the show."

"Let's not overreact," Sandy said. "We've gotten through some tight spots before. What we really need is to get some rest and start fresh tomorrow."

"You mean later this morning," Pekar said, correcting her.

She sighed. "Later this morning, then."

Security locked the place down for the night and posted guards outside the soundstage. Webb, O'Sullivan, and Pekar went home to catch what sleep they could before reporting to work in the morning. Pekar refused to go to the hospital to have his head looked at. "Who has time?" he said.

The Hardys and the Mortons were escorted back to their trailer by the studio guards.

"How bad do you think the studio situation really is?" Iola asked when they were alone.

"Pretty bad, I'd say," Frank said. "Webb and O'Sullivan took the damage to the sets in stride, but it's sure to hit the show in the pocketbook."

"Boy," Iola said, "things sure have been messed up since we got here."

"At least Sandy and Webb aren't blaming us for the troubles," Chet said.

"Not yet, anyway," Joe countered. "But they could. After all, Frank and I are the only ones who saw this intruder we fought."

"How did the real culprit get past the guards?" Chet asked.

"Clearly he knows the studio better than we do," Frank said. "We were lucky to catch him at all on the soundstage. If there'd been only one of us, he'd have gotten away scott free."

"And security isn't great at the studio," Joe said. "Probably that's one of the areas where they're saving money."

"Everything they're saving there, they're losing in sabotage and stolen goods," Iola said.

Frank and Joe both nodded. "There's nothing more we can do tonight," Frank said. "Maybe we'll have some new ideas in the morning."

"I'd settle for some old ideas," Chet said, "just so long as they explain what's going on around here."

The morning was gray and overcast. Chet woke up early for his makeup call, only to find that Peck Wilson had returned from the hospital. Chet's stint as the Slayer from Sirius was over.

Chet returned to the trailer and moped. "I'm out of showbiz before I've hardly begun!" he said.

"Go back to bed," Joe said sleepily. "You'll feel better after some more rest."

Neither Joe nor Frank could sleep after Chet came back and decided to get up. They ate a quick breakfast in the commissary, then headed to the set.

If the pace around the show had been heated

previously, this day it could only be described as feverish. Stagehands and technicians worked frantically to repair the damage to the sets.

Rod Webb had come up with a scheme to shoot around the damaged sets, and Sandy had rewritten some scenes to accommodate the changes. The dark-haired writer/creator looked as if she'd gotten little or no sleep.

Iola got made up as a different character again and did some more walk-throughs during scenes set in the ship's corridors and infirmary.

The show's actors had put aside their differences and were working smoothly as a unit, even the combative Geoff Gross.

"Probably he's happy to have me out of the Slayer suit," Chet said quietly.

"What about you?" Joe asked. "Still missing the hot lights?"

Chet shook his head. "Nah. Let Peck Wilson brawl with Gross next time. My bruises haven't healed yet."

During a break in shooting, Peck Wilson came over to congratulate Chet for his work in the show. "You really helped out," Wilson said. "And you don't look half-bad as the Slayer from Sirius. You might consider doing some stunt work when you get out of school."

Chet grinned. "Maybe you'll need an apprentice Slayer by then," he said.

Wilson laughed. "Let's hope the show lasts that long."

"We're just glad to have you back in action," Frank said. "The fire could have killed you."

"That's what they tell me," Wilson replied. "I don't remember much of what happened, to tell you the truth. I went over the hill and then—whammo!— Next thing I know, I wake up in the hospital."

"Did you slip and fall, or what?" Joe asked.

"I guess I must have," Wilson said. "I still have a big bump on the back of my head. I must have cracked my skull against a rock."

"Yeah, probably," Joe said, but the look he gave Frank said that he didn't believe it.

After Wilson went back to work, Frank said, "Are you thinking that he was probably hit from behind?"

"Yeah, just like Pekar—by the kung fu alien," Joe said.

"Why, though?" Chet asked.

"If we knew that, we'd have this mystery solved," Frank said.

The morning flew by with the crew shooting pages almost as quickly as the rewrites could be printed from Sandy's computer. When Jerri Bell and Claudia Rajiv finished their morning scenes, they invited Chet, Frank, and Joe to join them for lunch while Iola continued working.

"I don't see how we can make up for lost time

without shooting this weekend," Claudia said. "And even then, getting back to the park will be tricky."

"Maybe Sandy will rewrite those scenes," Iola suggested.

"Poor Sandy," Claudia said. "She's working herself to death."

"And the rest of us, too," Jerri said. She sighed and ran a hand through her blond hair. "I guess I'd better cancel my plans for Saturday and Sunday."

"The price of fame," Frank said.

Jerri smiled and laughed. "Listen to me!" she said. "The show's in trouble and I'm worried about a weekend getaway."

"I'd tell you to get a life, but I think that may be your problem," Claudia said.

Lunch soon ended, and the women went back to work. Frank, Joe, and Chet lingered for a few moments, finishing their desserts.

"Did you notice that Geoff Gross and Matt Stiller had their eyes on us the whole time Jerri was here?" Frank said.

Joe nodded. "And they left just as soon as Jerri and Claudia did."

"Well, it'll be harder for Gross to take a poke at me now that I'm out of the Slayer outfit," Chet said.

Shooting stretched late into the afternoon, with technicians and actors flying around in a state just short of chaos. Stiller kept busy running errands for the cast, especially Jerri Bell, and stayed out of the way of the Hardys and Mortons except to toss them an occasional sneer.

"He's an excellent gofer . . . for a creep," Iola commented.

"I don't think Gross is too pleased with him, though," Joe said. "Look."

As they watched, Geoff Gross drained the coffee cup in his hand and violently crushed it. He tossed it aside and called, "Stiller! Where's my coffee?"

Stiller looked annoyed but said, "Coming, Mr. Gross." He took his tray, piled high with coffee and soft drinks, and ducked behind a flat to cross to Gross's chair. Webb was working nearby, setting up the next shot. Suddenly he turned and yelled, "Hey! Look out!"

He rushed behind the flat, and a moment later there was a loud popping noise, and the lights on the set went out. Immediately, the emergency lights kicked on, and chaos erupted on the set.

Jerri Bell screamed, "Somebody call an ambulance!"

13 The Final Straw

Frank, Joe, and the others raced to the sound of Jerri's voice. They found her behind the flat, next to the prone body of Matt Stiller. He lay in a pool of spilled coffee, next to a fallen electrical cable. Stiller's eyes were wide open, and his body was shaking. His mouth moved, but no intelligible words came out.

Rod Webb, who had been standing next to a nearby circuit-breaker box, dashed to Stiller's side. "Is he all right?" Webb asked. "That cable must have fallen," he said. "I tried to warn him, but . . ."

Frank kneeled next to the quivering gofer. "It looks like he's had a pretty bad shock. We should keep him quiet until the EMTs get here."

"It's a good thing I knew where the breaker was,"

Webb said, wiping his sweaty forehead with the back of his sleeve.

"He might have been killed," Jerri said, tears streaming down her face. She held Stiller's hand and tried to calm him. Stiller's eyes darted around frantically, but he still couldn't talk.

A large group of cast and crew members began to gather. Joe stepped in and said, "Keep back, everybody. Give him room."

A few long minutes later the EMTs arrived. They quickly stabilized Stiller and put him on a gurney. As the emergency workers rolled Stiller out of the soundstage, he kept his hand clamped tightly around Jerri Bell's. She followed him out to the ambulance.

On the set, silence reigned for a few moments. Then Rod Webb spoke up. "I . . . I don't know what to say," he said. "Everyone take thirty. We've still got a schedule to meet."

Shaken, everyone quietly filed out of the stage. The Hardys and the Mortons retired to their trailer.

"Another accident," Iola moaned.

"I'm not buying it," Frank replied.

"If it wasn't an accident," Chet said, "how did the perpetrator set it up?"

"You'd need intimate knowledge of the cast and crew," Joe said. "For example, the alien we fought clearly knew the stage and sets better than we did."

They pondered the situation but came up with

no new ideas. Finally, Frank said, "The only thing we can do is keep our eyes open. Maybe whoever's doing this will tip his or her hand somehow."

They quietly made their way back to the sound-stage. When they arrived, they found Sandy, Rod Webb, Claudia, Bruce Reid, Peck Wilson, Ramon Torres, and a number of extras standing near the infirmary set. A larger circle of stagehands and crew members stood beyond the ring of cast members. In the center of the ring was a well-dressed man in a business suit.

The well-dressed man pushed his black-framed glasses up on his nose. "Some of you may know me," he said. "My name is Mr. Mycroft, and I work with the studio's business department."

He looked gravely at everyone gathered as he spoke. "As many of you are aware, *Warp Space* has had a number of difficulties lately—both with rat-ings and production. In light of today's accident, the insurance company has suspended our policy, pending a full review.

"With no insurance, we can't produce this series," Mycroft said. "Therefore, I am suspending produc-tion of *Warp Space* effective immediately. I'm very sorry. The main office will be in touch with all of you regarding settlement of your contracts."

"You . . . you mean we won't be starting up again?" Sandy O'Sullivan asked.

125

"I can't say for certain," Mycroft said, "but resuming production seems unlikely at this time."

Sandy's lower lip trembled, and she wiped tears from the corners of her eyes. Geoff Gross pounded his fist into one of the set's walls. Some members of the crew groaned and turned away. Rod Webb tensed. "We'll fight this," he said.

"You bet we will," said Bruce Reid. Claudia, Ramon Torres, and several others grumbled their agreement.

Mycroft took off his glasses and wiped them. "I'm sorry," he said. "There's nothing I can do. You should all go home and calm down. The main office will be in touch with every one of you shortly."

The mood in Stan Pekar's studio was as somber as on the rest of the lot when Iola went to have her makeup removed. Pekar and Nelson completed their jobs without much talk. Then Iola and the other crew members went their separate ways. The Hardys and Chet waited for Iola and walked back to the trailer with her.

Just before they went inside, Sandy O'Sullivan dashed up. Her eyes were red from crying.

"I am so sorry about this," she said. "It's not the kind of prize we had in mind for the contest."

Iola gave her a hug. "Oh, Sandy," she said, "don't worry about it. It's not your fault."

Sandy bit her lower lip to stop it from shaking.

"You can stay in the trailer the rest of the week, of course," she said. "And I want you to know that we'll find some alternate prize—perhaps an appearance on another UAN show."

"We're not much concerned with the prize at the moment," Chet said. "I just wish there was some way we could help."

Sandy shook her head. "There's nothing you can do," she said. "If it'll make you feel better, though, Claudia's still getting people together at her place in an hour or two because . . . well, I'm afraid it may feel more like a wake than a celebration."

"We'd be happy to come," Joe said.

"Wouldn't miss it," added Iola.

"Great," Sandy said. Fumbling with her purse, she pulled out a small photocopied sheet with directions on it and handed it to Iola. "We'll see you there, then," she said. "Keep your chins up."

"You, too," Chet said.

Sandy gave them a final weak smile. She dashed off toward the main studio building before her emotions could get the better of her.

Frank frowned. "There *is* something more we can do," he said.

Joe nodded. "We can get to the bottom of this mystery."

The Hardys and the Mortons poked around the lot as much as they could before the "party." They didn't find any clues, though, and their investigation was hampered by the police looking into the accident.

Around four o'clock, they piled into the van and drove to Claudia Rajiv's home in the northern suburbs of Jewel Ridge. Claudia's place was a new condo near the Jewel River. The home featured a split-level living room with a nice view of the river and the city skyline.

Jerri Bell, Bruce Reid, Peck Wilson, Ramon Torres, Marge Nelson, and a number of other cast and crew members were milling around aimlessly.

"Thanks for coming," Claudia said to the teens. "To tell you the truth, given what happened today, I wasn't sure if anyone would show up."

"How are you handling it?" Iola asked.

"Okay," Claudia said. "Better than a lot of the others. I'm sure I'll find more work, and I've got enough stashed away to pay my bills for the next year and a half."

Bruce Reid walked over to them, a drink in his hand. "Yes, Claudia, my dear," he said morosely, "I'm sure you'll land on your feet. I wish I could say the same for the rest of us."

"I can't believe they shut us down," Ramon Torres said. "We were doing good work."

"Money talks, Ramon," Reid replied. "Don't think it was anything else."

Jerri Bell stood up, her hands fiddling nervously

with a large ring of keys. "I can't believe that you're thinking about yourselves when poor Matt is in the hospital!" she said. "He could have been killed."

"I was nearly killed, too, remember?" Peck Wilson said. "Maybe shutting down for a while is the best thing to do. Maybe we'll have better luck if we make a fresh start."

Jerri looked as though she might burst into tears. Claudia walked over to her and gave her a hug. Both of them sat down on the large sectional sofa in the middle of the room. Iola, Chet, and the Mortons took seats nearby. The other members of the crew drifted into small groups and talked quietly among themselves.

"I'm sure Matt will be all right," Claudia said to Jerri.

"He . . . he just looked so scared when they took him away," Jerri said. "I felt so helpless." Her fingers continued to fiddle with the key ring as she spoke.

The Spacefleet insignia on the ring caught Iola's attention. "That's a nice key ring," she said, trying to get Jerri's mind off the accident. "Do you think I could get one like it as a souvenir?"

"This?" Jerri said. "It's not mine. Matt pressed it into my hand before they took him away. He said I should keep it until he got out of the hospital. At least, that's what I think he said. He was pretty delirious at the time."

"Wait a minute," Claudia said. "Matt gave you *that?* Can I look at it?"

Jerri nodded and handed the key ring to Claudia. The ring had keys of various shapes and sizes attached to a central Spacefleet insignia. Claudia's brow knitted together as she studied it.

"What's wrong?" Frank asked.

"This is one of the limited-edition key rings," Claudia said. "Only the people who were onboard when the show was greenlighted got one. Matt *wasn't* one of those people. Even Jerri didn't join the cast soon enough to get one."

"Then how'd Matt get it?" Joe asked.

"Maybe it's one of the things that went missing from the set," Frank said. "I wonder if Stiller knows anything about it. It might help the show if he did."

"But Matt's in the hospital," Jerri said, wiping a tear away. "You can't ask him."

"We wouldn't have to," Joe said, catching on to Frank's plan. "If you'll lend us that key ring, we can check out his apartment. He might have been doing some investigating on his own."

"Then we might know if that electrical shock Stiller got was really an accident, or if someone meant to hurt him," Frank said. "We might even discover what he was trying to tell you."

"Well, okay," Jerri said. "So long as you get the keys back to me before morning. Matt might want them tomorrow, if he's feeling better."

130

"No problem," Joe said. He took the keys and headed for the door.

"Sorry we can't stay," Frank said to Claudia. "I just hope we'll have good news the next time we see you."

"I hope so, too," Claudia said.

A quick check of the phone book turned up an address for Matt Stiller. He lived in an apartment close to the studio. The blanket of clouds made the evening almost as dark as night by the time Frank parked the van in front of Stiller's building.

"Won't the police have Stiller's place sealed off?" Chet asked as they went to find the apartment.

"The police think that Stiller's getting shocked was an accident," Frank said. "They'd have no reason to seal the apartment."

In short order they found the right door, opened it, and stepped inside. The floor of the apartment was covered with papers, clothes, and other personal items.

"What a mess!" Iola said. "How can he live like this?"

"This is no normal mess," Frank said. "Someone's ransacked the place."

Joe pointed to the window. "And there he is!"

14 The Secret Number

Sure enough, a fleeting shadow moved across the surface of Stiller's first-floor window. Joe and Frank dashed toward the window and threw it open.

As they peered out into the darkness, they caught a brief glimpse of a figure disappearing into the lush landscaping.

Joe pounded his fist on the window. "No way we could find him," he said.

"Could you see who it was?" Chet asked.

Frank shook his head. "No, he was much too far away, but this confirms that something rotten is going on with the show. It's too big a coincidence that Stiller's apartment should be broken into otherwise."

"Do you think he got what he was looking for?" Iola asked.

"No way to tell," Joe replied. "We'll just have to look around a bit and see what we turn up."

Papers littered the floor of the efficiency apartment. The drawers of the dresser had been turned out and the clothes scattered. The closets had been rifled, too, and their contents spilled. A smashed computer lay atop the other items, but everything else seemed intact. Among the refuse was a large number of *Warp Space* souvenirs.

"Look at all this stuff!" Joe said. "It looks like a retail store."

"I've never seen some of these items before," Iola said, "and I checked up on *Warp Space* collectibles before we came to the shoot."

Frank poked amid the action figures, T-shirts, script pages, badges, toys, and other paraphernalia. "This stuff must have cost Stiller a bundle," he said. "Or . . ."

"Or Matt Stiller was responsible for the thefts around the lot," Joe said, finishing Frank's idea.

"It makes sense," Frank said. "In his position as gofer, he'd have access to most parts of the soundstage and offices. We were told that a lot of promotional items, like the toys, kept disappearing from the studio."

"And he'd know where they were working, and where it would be 'safe' to steal stuff from," said Iola.

Frank nodded. "The question is, why did he take all this?"

"There are a lot of online auction printouts here," Iola said, holding up a sheaf of computer paper. "I'd say he was researching the market."

"So Stiller was stealing the stuff to sell online," Chet said. "What a creep. I'm almost happy that he's in the hospital."

"Stiller being a thief doesn't answer all our questions, though," Frank said. "For instance, why did he cause the accidents?"

"Maybe to cover up his other crimes," Joe suggested. "Take a look at this." He handed Frank a small star-shaped insignia pin. "Isn't this the medal that was missing from the Slayer from Sirius costume?"

"Yeah," Chet said. "That's the one they had to replace when I took over for Peck Wilson. You think Stiller knocked Peck out just to steal it?"

"And set the fire to cover it up," Frank said.

Iola rummaged through the papers some more. "Here's some script pages from that same day," she said.

Joe began searching, too. "And here's some correspondence to other collectors," he said. "Stiller was using a pseudonym for his inquiries, but apparently he thought that the value of his collection would go up if the show went off the air."

"Rarity does affect price," Frank said. "If the show went out of production, they'd stop making collectibles. Therefore, everything associated with

Warp Space would become more valuable."

"That is so *cold*," Iola said.

"Here's the clincher," Joe said, picking up a fallen trophy from the floor. "It's for a kung fu tournament. I'd say the alien we fought on the soundstage was really Stiller wearing the mask he stole from Pekar."

"Where's the mask, though?" Frank asked. "I don't see it here."

"Maybe the burglar took it," Chet suggested.

"But why take only that one item rather than the computer, or something more valuable?" Iola asked.

"This place is a treasure trove of valuable *Warp Space* collectibles, if a thief was looking to cash in," Chet added.

"Maybe he didn't know what the *Warp Space* stuff was worth," Joe said. "Or maybe we interrupted him, and he didn't have time to take anything more."

Frank shook his head. "No. If he'd found what he wanted, he wouldn't have waited around to be discovered. He must have been looking for something specific and didn't find it—at least not quickly. Why rifle the apartment otherwise?"

"So, what the burglar wanted might still be here somewhere," Iola said.

"The only way to find out," Joe said, "is to keep looking."

"Do you think he smashed the computer to conceal evidence?" Chet asked.

"Probably," Frank said. "But we have no way of recovering whatever was on the hard drive. I'm afraid we'll just have to do this the old-fashioned way."

So the four of them rooted through the items strewn about the apartment, looking for any clues to the burglar's identity or objective. After three-quarters of an hour, Iola turned something up at the bottom of a pile of papers.

"There are some e-mails here to Stiller," she said. "Whoever wrote them seems to be encouraging Stiller to cause trouble on the set. They're filled with rants about rich, spoiled actors who deserve whatever trouble they get."

Joe looked at the paper. "The return address is a Yipmail account. That makes it harder."

"Why?" Chet asked.

"Because the service is free," Joe said, "and you can access it from any computer. It's a perfect way to send anonymous e-mail. I've heard of con artists setting up dozens of phony accounts in as many different names to bilk their marks."

"Stiller was using a Yipmail account, too," Iola said.

"So that's a dead end," Frank said.

"I'd assume that the writer might be one of the cast or crew," Joe said. "Certainly Stiller didn't try to electrocute himself, and I doubt he could have been behind *all* the other problems."

"It seems like a lot of mayhem for one guy to cause," Chet agreed.

Joe jangled Stiller's key ring, running his fingers through the various-size keys. "Hey," he said, "what if Stiller had another place to stash his stolen goods?"

"Like, where, Joe?" Iola asked.

Joe held up a single key from the ring. It had a bright red plastic haft with the number 878 printed on it in white letters. "What's this look like to you?" he asked.

"The locker key from a bus or train station," Chet said. "But that could be anywhere."

"I don't think so," Frank said, "he'd want a locker that would be convenient to use."

"The studio lot!" Iola said. "There are lockers there. I've seen them near the cafeteria."

Frank nodded. "That would be logical. Stiller could stash items there to take home later."

"Or he could store them there if they were too hot to smuggle out of the studio," Chet added. "Like when the guards were alerted last night."

"I think we need to look inside that locker," Joe said.

By eight-thirty the Hardys and Mortons had returned to the studio. Because their prize gave them the studio trailer for the rest of the week, they had no trouble with the guards at the gate. A gentle rain had begun to fall, and the lot was quiet and dark, save for a single light in the production building. The guard told them that Sandy was working late.

Since *Warp Space* had been shut down, the cafeteria was deserted. It didn't take the teens long to find locker 878 in a row outside the building. The locker was about the size of a large breadbox, big enough for about two backpacks. Joe fitted the key into the lock, and opened the metal door.

Inside lay the blue alien mask, a sheaf of stolen script pages, and a number of other, small *Warp Space* trinkets. One in particular caught the detectives' attention.

"A Spacefleet pager!" Iola said. "I've read about these. They're very rare."

"It would probably fetch big bucks on the collectibles market," Chet said.

"It might fetch us more than that," Frank said. "It might be the key to this mystery."

"How?" Chet and Iola asked simultaneously.

"Look at these script pages," Joe said, rifling through them. "They're all dated today."

"That and the tight security last night means that everything Stiller took recently—within the last twenty-four hours—should still be in here," Frank said.

"Like the mask," Iola said.

"Stiller never got the chance to take them home because he nearly got electrocuted," Chet added.

"Right," said Joe. "Unless the rifling of Stiller's apartment is just coincidence—"

"And I'm beginning to think that *nothing* in this case is coincidence," Frank put in.

"The burglar who rifled through Stiller's apartment must have known Stiller wouldn't be there," Joe continued. "The intruder could even be the same person who tried to kill Stiller. Since the burglar didn't find what he was looking for, it's possible what he wanted is in this locker. That's our best lead, anyway."

"It can't be the pages," Frank said, continuing his brother's thought, "and it's probably not the mask. Stan Pekar can make more of those."

"Which leaves the pager," Chet said. "But even if it's valuable as a collector's item, why would that be so important? Why would someone try to electrocute Stiller for it?"

"It might not be the pager," Joe said, "but what's in the pager's memory." He pressed the recall button and a number popped up. "Do you have our cell phone, Frank?"

Frank nodded and pulled the phone out. He dialed the number and switched the phone to its speaker function.

"You've reached the office of David August, senior

producer at Monumental Broadcasting," said a voice on the other end of the line. "If you're a hotshot with a deal that can't wait, leave your name and number, we'll get back to you as soon as possible. *Beep!*"

Frank switched the phone off.

"So, it's sabotage by a competitor," Chet said. "Somebody here is working for Monumental Broadcasting."

"*Warp Space* is a new show," Joe said. "It can't be that much of a threat to another network. Despite its cult following, the show's ratings aren't great."

"I think," Frank said, "it all boils down to who, besides Stiller, might benefit if the series went under. And how that person ties into Monumental Broadcasting."

"But how can we figure that out?" Iola said.

"We can talk to Sandy O'Sullivan for starters," Joe said.

It didn't take the four friends long to walk through the rain to Sandy's office. They knocked on the door, and when there was no answer they went inside.

The found the young writer/producer slumped over her desk. She looked exhausted, and her face was stained with tears. She wiped her red cheeks with her sleeve as the group came in. "Oh!" she said, "I'm sorry. I didn't know you were here." She began to aimlessly straighten the papers on her desk. "I've got so much to do, just to shut this place down." Her lower lip quivered and she bit it to keep from crying.

"Sandy," Frank said, "we're sorry about the show. We're also pretty convinced that *Warp Space* has been a victim of deliberate sabotage."

"Sabotage?" Sandy said, confused. "That's crazy. Who would sabotage the show—and why?"

"We're hoping to find out," Joe said, "and we need your help. Before we can find the saboteur, though, we need to ask a strange favor."

"What?"

Joe looked directly into her eyes. "Can we see your Spacefleet pager, please?" he asked.

Sandy looked puzzled, but she said, "Um . . . sure. I have it right here." She pulled a pager, just like the one they'd found in the locker, from her belt.

Joe and Frank looked at each other and smiled. "We're glad you have that," Frank said. "It proves you're not the person behind all this trouble. Can you tell us who else has these pagers?"

"Sure," Sandy said. "Stan Pekar, Rod Webb, Claudia Rajiv, Peck Wilson, Bruce Reid, Geoff Gross, and two of the UAN execs who green-lighted the show."

"Good," Joe said. "Now, we need two more things. We need e-mail addresses for all those people, and we need to take a look at their *Warp Space* contracts.

"That would be highly irregular," Sandy said. "I don't think I could show you, legally."

"It might save the show," Frank said.

Sandy looked so torn that they feared she might break down again.

"Tell you what," Joe said. "We'll tell you what we're looking for, and you can check the contracts for us."

Sandy bit her lip again. "Um, I like you guys, and you've been very helpful," she said. "But how do I know I can trust you?"

"You can call Officer Con Riley at the Bayport PD," Frank said. "He'll vouch for our integrity. We promise not to reveal any contract details you divulge to us." Frank wrote Con's number on a piece of paper and handed it to Sandy.

"All right," she said. "If you guys check out, I'll tell you what you want to know. Can you step out of the office for a moment while I make the call?"

"Sure thing," Joe said. He and the others stepped outside and closed the door.

"What do we do after Con vouches for you?" Iola asked.

"First," Frank said, "we check those contracts. Then we set a trap for a saboteur."

15 The Message from Space

A few minutes later Sandy reopened the door.

"Well," she said, "it looks like you're on the level." She handed Frank a piece of paper. "Here are the e-mail addresses you need. Come on in, I'll show you the contracts."

"Great," Joe said. "And could you do us one more favor?"

"Sure."

"Could you get in touch with the people on that list in about forty-five minutes and have them check their e-mail?" Joe asked.

"Okay, but why?"

"Just tell them that you got a nasty flame and you're wondering if they got the same garbage or if you should report it to the police," Frank said. "It'd be best if you called them from home."

Sandy nodded. "Okay. So long as you call me immediately if your suspicions pan out."

"Sure thing," Joe said. "Now, tell us about those contracts. Then we'll need to send some e-mail."

"You can use my computer after I've gone," Sandy said.

By nine-thirty the teens had checked the contracts, and Sandy had gone home to make her calls.

"What now?" Iola asked.

"We're going to send an e-mail to the suspects in the case, demanding a ransom for the pager and the number it contains," Frank said. "We'll set up a meeting for midnight, and the person who shows up will be our criminal."

"We think we know who it is," Joe said typing on Sandy's computer, "but we need to erase any doubt. I'll take a couple of minutes to set up a phony Yip-mail account for us to use, then we're golden."

"That's why you told Sandy to call the suspects and have them check their e-mail," Chet said.

Joe winked at him. "Bingo. You'll make rocket scientist yet."

"I'd settle for TV star," Chet said.

Frank and Joe took turns at working the computer for about fifteen minutes while Iola and Chet looked on.

"There," Joe said. "The trap is set. Now all we have to do is wait."

Chet folded his arms over his chest. "Waiting is the hardest part."

Midnight was still two hours away when the Hardys finished their setting up their blackmail scheme. They chose *Warp Space*'s bridge set for the ransom drop. They went to the bridge immediately after locking up Sandy's office and set up a stakeout. They went over the set and the surrounding areas carefully, making sure that the saboteur wouldn't be able to outmaneuver them.

With an hour and a half to go, they selected places to hide and divided the tasks needed to make the trap work. They turned off all the regular lights so that only the displays on the consoles illuminated the room. Dim lighting was essential to their plan. Illumination from the multicolored control panels gave the set an eerie glow.

"I'll stand by the cell phone and hit the lights when we catch the saboteur," Iola said. "The fire alarm is right by the light switch, so I can pull that in case we need help."

"Sounds good," said Joe.

"I'll block the elevator exit," Chet said. The carpenters hadn't finished reassembling the set's fake elevator after Joe's brawl. Thus, it was an obvious avenue for escape. "There's plenty of carpentry stuff and flats back there for me to hide behind."

"I'll wait near the main entrance to the set, where they put the cameras," Joe said. "That leaves the decoy job to you, Frank."

Frank nodded and pulled the blue alien mask over his face. "We'll have a bit of an advantage if the saboteur thinks I'm Stiller. The low lights will help with that deception," he said, taking up a position near the bridge's command chair.

Chet checked his watch. "We've still got an hour and fifteen minutes left, guys," he said.

"If I were the criminal," Joe said, "I'd get here early, to try to catch the blackmailer by surprise."

"Yeah," Chet said. "That makes sense. I just hope I can stay awake. I've been working long hours lately, you know."

"In space, no one can hear you snore," Frank said.

The rest of the group chuckled. As the sound of their laughter died away, the soundstage door creaked open.

"They're early!" Iola whispered.

Joe shook his head. "We're set," he said. "Everyone take your places." He melted into the shadows near the front of the set. Chet quickly exited through the elevator. Iola followed him out and took her position near the fire alarm, fairly close to her brother.

They all kept still, trying to make as little noise as possible. A few moments later they heard voices coming their way. "There are two of them!" Iola whispered. Chet nodded.

Frank sat patiently in the command chair, waiting for the saboteur to arrive.

The voices grew louder, and the sound of footsteps echoed through the darkness. A moment later Bruce Reid and Jerri Bell walked into the dim light of the control room.

"Not the end of the world," Reid finished.

"That's easy for you to say," the young actress replied. "You've been in a bunch of shows before. I may never recover if my first role is a flop."

"The role's not a flop," Reid said. "You're great in it. People know that there are good actors on shows that don't get renewed."

Suddenly the two of them stopped and peered into the shadows where Frank was sitting. "Stan? Is that you?" Reid asked.

Joe stepped out of the darkness, "No," he said. "It's Frank and Joe Hardy."

"What are you guys doing here?" Reid asked.

"We might ask you the same thing," Chet said as he stepped out of the elevator.

Jerri Bell glanced around nervously. "We were feeling bad about the show," she said.

"We left the party and decided to take a walk to clear our heads," Bruce continued. "We came down here to have one last look around."

"Then you're not interested in the pager?" Iola

asked, coming through the elevator door and standing next to her brother.

"What pager?" Jerri and Reid asked simultaneously.

Frank, still in his alien disguise, stood up. "I'm not surprised," he said. "We weren't expecting them."

"You mean you were meeting someone here?" Jerri asked. "Who?"

"The person who sabotaged the show, we hope," Joe said. "You two need to get out of here, or you'll spoil our trap."

"Spoil nothing," Reid said excitedly. "Is there anything we can do to help?"

"We don't have time to add new cast members into our screenplay," Frank said. "The best thing you can do is get out of here. We don't want the saboteur getting suspicious."

Reid nodded slowly. "Okay," he said. "If that's all we can do. Come on, Jerri. We'll go back to the party. You can reach us there if you catch whoever it is."

"Fair enough," Joe said. "Keep your fingers crossed."

"We will," Jerri said. She and Reid turned and left quickly.

"Well," Chet said after they'd gone, "that got the old adrenaline pumping."

"Let's try to settle down again," Frank said. "The

night's early yet." The teens returned to their stations and waited quietly.

Three quarters of an hour later, they heard the stage door creak open again. This time, though, no talking followed the noise, only soft footfalls on the concrete floor.

As the teens waited tensely, a shadowy figure crept through the darkness toward the bridge set. When he got there, he spotted Frank sitting in the command chair. The person stood at the edge of the set, just out of range of the dim light from the consoles.

"Stiller?" said the intruder. "I thought you were still in the hospital. Taking my pager was a mistake."

"I've been expecting you," Frank said, making his voice hoarse so that the saboteur wouldn't realize he wasn't Stiller. "Why don't you step into the light, Mr. Webb."

Rod Webb stepped forward, so that he could be seen clearly. "So," the director said, "you figured out it was me, even after I fed you all that information to make you think it was Jerri Bell encouraging your vandalism and petty theft. I'm impressed. I didn't think you had that many brains."

"You'd be surprised what I know," Frank said in his alien voice. "I know that you're not making much money on this assignment. You did it just to fill out your contract, betting that the show would fold quickly. When it didn't, you decided to help it along. Too bad. You could have made some real money if *Warp Space* took off."

"Who could wait that long?" Webb said. "You certainly didn't want to. Did you think I was feeding you all that juicy info for your own benefit? Did you think I didn't know who was behind all the petty thievery? I knew you were causing accidents, hoping to drive up the prices of collectibles. I turned my back on what you did because you and I *both* wanted the show off the air. If the show flew, I'd have been locked in for another three years. Why should I waste my best years on this penny-ante network? This way, we both make out."

"Maybe you do," Frank said, playing his Stiller part to the hilt. "I'm not so lucky. When my loot runs out I get to be a gofer on another show. At least, that's how it *might* have been, if you hadn't tried to kill me."

Webb shrugged. "What else could I do?" he said. "When my pager went missing, I knew you'd taken it. I couldn't chance you stumbling onto my connection to Monumental Broadcasting. They're lining up a sweet deal for me—a deal I can't pass up. It was just my bad luck that you hid the pager before I zapped you."

He walked casually toward the command chair. Frank stood as he approached.

"Too bad," Webb said. "A smart guy like you should have figured if I tried to kill you once, I wouldn't hesitate a second time." He drew a gun from his pocket and pointed it at Frank.

"Now, Iola!" Chet called.

At the sound of her brother's voice, Iola switched on the big floodlights. The blazing display dazzled Webb for a moment. In that instant Joe rushed forward and knocked the gun from the director's hand. Frank aimed a punch at Webb's chin, but the director stepped back, away from the blow. As Chet Morton charged in through the elevator door, Webb leaned against the bridge control panel and stabbed one of the buttons.

Foosh! The panel blew up in a huge shower of sparks. The Hardys and Chet staggered back. Webb tossed a console chair into Chet's midsection and fled. Chet went down, but Frank and Joe recovered and ran after the saboteur. The director bolted straight for the stage door with the brothers in hot pursuit.

As they ran, Joe spotted a long cable snaking along the floor from one set to the next. "Hey, Frank!" he said, pointing.

"Go for it," Frank said. "I'll catch him when he falls."

Joe reached down and grabbed the cable in both hands. He reeled back and cracked it like a whip. The cable snaked out in front of Webb, tripping him. The director fell sprawling to the floor, and before he could get up Frank caught him and clouted him in the jaw.

Webb went out like a light.

Frank smiled and pulled off his borrowed mask. "Good work, Joe," he said.

The sound of police sirens echoing through the open stage door told the brothers that Iola had done her job. She and Chet soon caught up with the Hardys. Together, they found some spare electrical cord and used it to tie Webb up.

"He who lives by the cable, dies by the cable," Joe said with a grin.

Two days later the cast and crew of *Warp Space* gathered at Claudia Rajiv's condo for a far happier party.

"Well," Sandy O'Sullivan said, hanging up her cell phone, "it's official. We've been saved from cancellation."

The assembled crew gave a whoop of approval.

"I guess the network figured the publicity from all this would offset the production losses," Bruce Reid said. "Good thing, too. I don't think my career could have stood another flop."

"What I don't understand," Claudia said to the Hardys, "is how you figured out it was Webb behind everything."

"I thought it was suspicious," Frank said, "that in

both Iola's accident and Stiller's, that Webb knew exactly what to do to cut the power. The evening we caught Webb, I remembered Millani saying that Webb had started in showbiz as a gaffer's assistant."

"Because gaffers work the lights and electrical equipment on a set," Joe said, "Webb knew just how to sabotage the control panels and Chet's ray gun, among other things. He also arranged the 'accident' that zapped Stiller and one that nearly hurt Iola. Stiller was behind what happened to Peck Wilson, though, as well as a lot of the other mischief around the sets. Webb secretly encouraged him, hoping to drive the show under."

"Killing the show would have allowed Webb to move west and take on a new assignment for Monumental Broadcasting," Frank said. "The number on the stolen pager was to a producer's office. It seemed unlikely that a big dealmaker like David August would be calling anyone below the level of producer or director."

"That narrowed it down to Webb or Sandy," Joe said. "But Sandy had nothing to gain if the show went under, and everything to lose. That left Webb. We didn't have proof, though, until he came to the set."

"He'd wiped out Stiller's computer, and anything else that might have led back to him," Chet said.

"But he didn't get the pager," Iola said, "and that's what nailed him."

"I can't get over how bad I felt for that creep Stiller!" Jerri Bell said.

"He got what he deserved," Stan Pekar said, rubbing the back of his head where Stiller had hit him.

"In any case," Frank said. "I'm sure that both Stiller and Webb will be locked up for a long time."

"In the same cell, if there's any justice," Claudia Rajiv added.

Sandy O'Sullivan sighed. "I really don't know how I can thank all of you," she said. "If not for you four, *Warp Space* might have been space dust."

"Just doing our job," Joe said with a smile.

"Are you sure you won't take some more bit parts on the show?" Sandy asked.

"No, thanks," Iola said. "All that makeup was murder on my skin. No offense, Mr. Pekar."

"None taken," Stan Pekar replied.

Frank shook his head, too. "I think Joe and I have had our fifteen minutes of fame," he said.

"What about you, Chet?" Sandy O'Sullivan asked.

Chet Morton looked at his watch. "I might give it another go," he said. "If what they say is true about everybody getting fifteen minutes of fame, I figure I've got about fourteen minutes to go."